I
96

J
398.2   Gordon, Tulo.
Gor   Milbi : aboriginal
          tales from

Y0-CJF-781

$1765
B
068

MILBI

MILBI

Aboriginal Tales from
Queensland's Endeavour River

Told and illustrated by Tulo Gordon
Translation by John B. Haviland

AUSTRALIAN NATIONAL UNIVERSITY PRESS
A DIVISION OF PERGAMON PRESS AUSTRALIA

Australian National University Press is a division of Pergamon Press (Australia) and a member of the Pergamon Group of Companies.

AUSTRALIA	Pergamon Press (Australia) Pty Ltd, 19a Boundary Street, Rushcutters Bay, N.S.W. 2011, Australia
U.K.	Pergamon Press Ltd, Headington Hill Hall, Oxford OX3 0BW, England
U.S.A.	Pergamon Press Inc., Maxwell House, Fairview Park, Elmsford, N.Y. 10523, U.S.A.
CANADA	Pergamon Press Canada Ltd, Suite 104, 150 Consumer's Road, Willowdale, Ontario M2J 1P9, Canada
FEDERAL REPUBLIC OF GERMANY	Pergamon Press GmbH, 6242 Kronberg-Tanus Hammerweg 6, Postfach 1305, Federal Republic of Germany

First published in Australia in 1980 by the Australian National University Press. Reprinted in 1986

© Paintings, Tulo Gordon
   Translation, Tulo Gordon and John B. Haviland 1980

This book was published with the support of the Aboriginal Arts and Literature Boards of the Australia Council

National Library of Australia
Cataloguing-in-Publication entry

Gordon, Tulo.
   Milbi.

ISBN 0 08 032938 1.

1. Aborigines, Australian — Legends — Juvenile literature. 2. Legends — Australia — Juvenile literature. I. Haviland, John B. (John Beard). II. Title.

398.2'0994

Library of Congress No. 79-53376

All Rights Reserved. No part of this publication may be reproduced, stored in a retrieval system or transmitted in any form or by any means, electronic, mechanical, photocopying, recording or otherwise without the prior permission of Pergamon Press (Australia) Pty Ltd.

Work on this collection of stories began in 1977 when my family and I worked at Hopevale Mission, living with my friend Billy Jacko and members of his household. The Australian Institute of Aboriginal Studies and the Department of Anthropology, Research School of Pacific Studies, Australian National University, supported this fieldwork, and funded Tulo Gordon's trip to Canberra in February and March of 1979, during which time we completed the manuscript and illustrations for this book.

John B. Haviland
Canberra, May 1979

Typeset by Queensland Type Service Pty. Ltd.
Designed by Kirsty Morrison
Printed in Singapore by
Singapore National Printers (Pte) Ltd.

Contents

Mungurru, the Scrub Python, and the Endeavour River	1
Dyiibuul, the bat	5
How Gudyal, the Eagle, got his wings	7
Ganhaar, the crocodile, and his wife	9
The giant Dindurr eel	13
How the giant Nhinhinhi fish changed the languages	17
The two night owl sisters and their Leichhardt tree	19
The old woman and her grandson on a lonely island	23
The forest spirit and his ten beautiful daughters	25
Frill Lizard and the honey	29
Durrgin, the water rat	33
Fog and Thunderstorm	37
The giant dingo dog	43
The two Dugul sisters	47
The big dance and the angry old woman	52
Behind the Myths	55

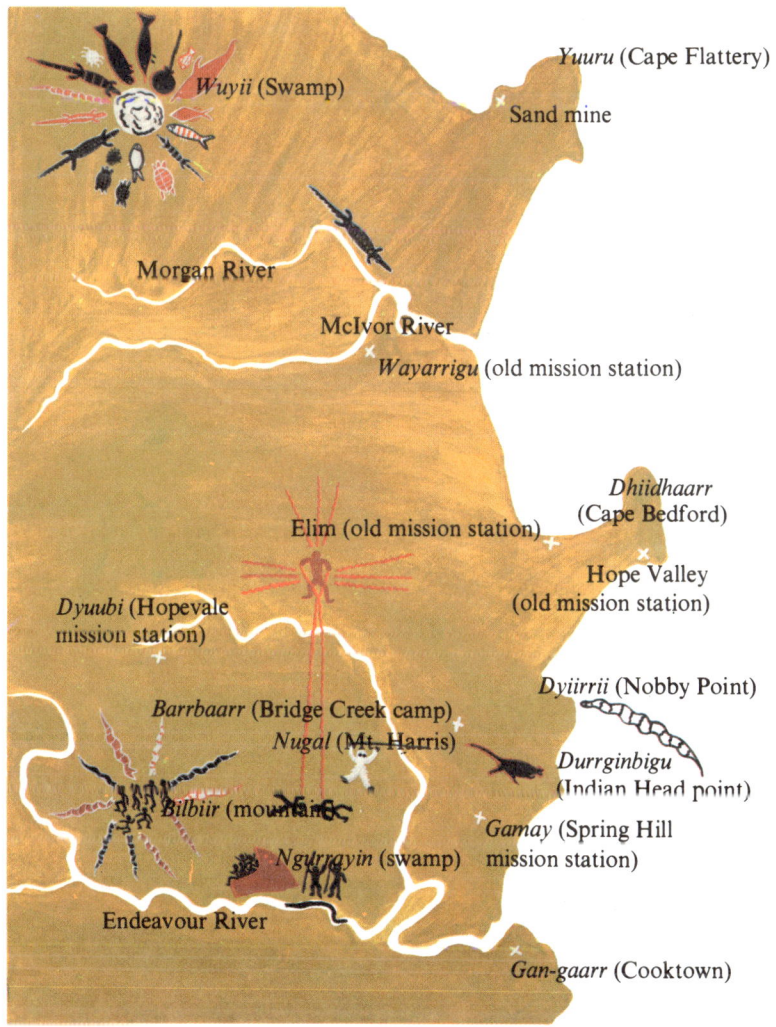

Mungurru, the Scrub Python, and the Endeavour River

There was a blackbird, called Dyirimadhi, who wanted to marry the daughter of old Mungurru, the Scrub Python. But that old Mungurru wouldn't give his daughter to Blackbird. He didn't want them to get married.

So Blackbird got cross with that old Scrub Python.

One day Scrub Python went out to sun himself. He lay down and stretched himself out in the heat of the day. Soon he fell asleep.

Dyirimadhi, the blackbird, had been out hunting. He was just on his way back to camp, when he heard some little birds laughing at something.

'What are these little birds laughing at', he said. 'Let me just go have a look.'

He went over quietly and saw that old Python sunning himself. The little birds were laughing at him, asleep in the sun.

'Ohh,' said Dyirimadhi, 'that's my old father-in-law. That's the fellow who didn't give me his daughter.'

So he went off quietly again, and he looked all around. He looked and he looked and he looked until he found a big, heavy stone. He took that big stone, and he flew way up high into the clouds with it. He flew around and then he looked down to see where that old Mungurru was lying. When he was right above him, he let go of the big stone.

The big stone went down, down, and landed right where old Python's head was. And you know, whenever you see a Scrub Python nowadays, he's got a flat head, from when that rock hit him.

When that big rock landed on his head, that old Mungurru started to thrash about. He rolled this way, then he rolled over that way. He didn't know what to do with all the pain.

Then the thought of the sea came into his mind. He headed off to the East, running towards the sea. He went straight down and came upon the sea right at Gan.garr, where Cooktown is today. He left deep tracks behind him, and that's where the Endeavour River is now. Before that old Scrub Python travelled down to the sea there was no river there.

When he reached the sea, old Mungurru went right out into the deep water. There he stayed for three nights and three days.

But the sea was very cold. That old Python began to feel cold right through, so he said to himself, 'I'll go back West again.'
He began to swim. He came to the shallow water, and then right up on the shore. Then he coiled himself up in the sand, and went to sleep.
Soon the early morning sun came up, and he was still asleep.

The sun rose and went higher and higher in the sky. Soon it was straight overhead, and still that old Mungurru slept. The sun became very very hot. It began to turn that Scrub Python hard. Finally the sun just turned him into a rock. Old Mungurru is still there, all coiled up, a big rock just beside the sea. The old people call that rock Dyiirrii. In English it is called Nobby Point.

Dyiibuul, the bat

This is a story about a little boy. His father and his mother died. So he was left in the care of his old grandfather. They used to stay in the same camp.

One day, the old grandfather got up and took his galga, his long hunting spear, and his spear-thrower. Then he went out hunting for game. He walked and he walked, and by and by he speared a big buck kangaroo, called galgaranggurr.

The old man came home, and he threw that big kangaroo down on the ground. Then he started to make an earth oven to cook it. He dug a hole in the ground, and he put sticks and big pieces of ant bed in it. Then he set fire to the wood, and when it got very hot, he put on more wood and threw that kangaroo on top. Then he covered the whole thing over with earth, and left the meat to cook.

He was tired out from hunting and making that gurrma, that earth oven. So the old man lay down to sleep.

While the old man was sleeping, that little boy was playing all over the camp, running here and there. But then he started to feel hungry. He tried to wake his grandfather

He tried to rouse him. 'Get up, get up, grandfather!' he said. But the old man was dead sleepy, and he wouldn't wake up

So the little boy got up, and went over to where the meat was cooking. He opened the gurrma a little bit, scraping off some of the dirt. Then he reached in and broke off one of that big kangaroo's ribs. It was already properly cooked. Then the little boy began to eat it.

While the boy was eating that kangaroo rib, the smell of the meat came over to his grandfather. The old man could smell the meat, and by and by his eyes opened and he looked around.

'Say, that little boy is eating my meat,' he said, and he got very angry, because he wanted the meat for himself.

He jumped up and went over to where the little boy was sitting down. Then he grabbed the kangaroo rib bone from the boy's hand, and he threw it way up in the air. That rib bone flew up and up, straight up, until it stuck right in the clouds. It became a new moon in the sky.

Then the old man turned around and boxed that little boy's ears.

The boy cried with pain, and he started to run away. He ran and ran, faster and faster, with the old man chasing him, chasing him, chasing along behind. The closer the old man got, the faster the boy ran.

As he ran along, the little boy began to grow wings. Two wings grew up on his back, and the boy began to fly.

His grandfather stopped and stood watching as the little fellow flew higher and higher.

He flew higher and higher, right up to the mountain side. There he found a cave and he flew inside.

You see, that little boy changed into a bat, and he lives in a cave right to the present day.

How Gudyal the Eagle, got his wings

Gudyal, the Eagle, lived way up on the mountain side. That's where his house was. He was very brave, and he was also a great hunter.

He used to go out hunting and kill all kinds of animals for meat. Then he would bring it home and give it all to the other people in the camp, especially the old ones and the sick people, who couldn't hunt for themselves.

Eagle was also very handsome.

In that same camp lived the two magpie sisters, and they used to watch that old Eagle. They saw that he was a really great hunter. By and by they fell in love with him. 'Ah,' they said to each other, 'let's go and marry him.'

Well, it wasn't long before Eagle married both those magpie sisters; he made them his wives.

After they were married, Eagle again began to go out hunting for meat, just as usual. Every day he would bring home a great lot of meat.

One night those two magpie sisters came to Eagle and told him that they were feeling sick in the stomach, from eating meat all the time. They'd had enough of meat.

The next morning they said, 'We're going to go out and look for some grubs and bring them home.'

'All right,' said Eagle, 'go on.'

The two magpie sisters went out and soon they found some bunggaga grubs at the base of a grass tree. They gathered more grubs all day long, and they brought a lot of grubs home in the evening.

They built a big fire. They put the grubs in the ashes, and covered them up to let them get cooked. Whey they were ready, the sisters took the grubs and ate some of them. They put the rest down for Eagle, their husband, to eat.

Soon Eagle came home, feeling very hungry. His wives said to him, 'Look, here are some bunggaga grubs for you to eat.' They set the food before him, and he sat down to eat.

Eagle was so hungry that he ate the grubs very quickly. But one of those grubs was already changing into a beetle. It had just begun to sprout wings. Eagle was eating in such a rush that he ate that one, too.

Suddenly, while he was sitting there, wings began to grow on his own back. They grew and grew and got big, until finally old Eagle stood up and flew right up in the air. He flew up and up, right up to the clouds.

And even today old Gudyal the Eagle has wings to fly around with.

Ganhaarr, the crocodile, and his wife

The old people say that Ganhaarr, the crocodile, is very cunning. And he is always on the lookout for a woman that he can steal away as his wife.

There was a big crocodile who lived down on the Endeavour River. Nearby there was a big camp of people, too. Every day all the young girls in that camp would go down to the river. They would go for a swim, and they would also hunt for mussels.

One day all the young girls were swimming around, gathering lots and lots of mussels. There was also a young woman from the camp, who had a little baby. She went down to the river with the others, and she sat right on the edge of the water, holding her baby in her arms.

All right, this big crocodile knew all the people were in the river. He came along and rose up out of the water where he could watch them. Then he swam along under the water. He passed all those other girls by, just left them alone. Instead he went straight for that young woman with her new baby. When he came close, he came up and grabbed that woman, with her baby. He threw them onto his back and jumped back into the water. Then he dived straight down, and swam right to his home, in a cave under the bank. He took them underground with him.

9

Well, that old Ganhaarr made that woman his wife, you see. But he was very jealous and suspicious. Every day, when the sun got hot he used to go out on the bank to sun himself. And he would take his wife along with him, too.

That crocodile would stretch out in the sun but he wouldn't go to sleep. He always kept one eye open, watching the woman. He wouldn't let that woman go away. If she tried to sneak away on him, he would run after her and catch her back again. When the sun cooled off, he would take her back to his underground home again.

The next time he came out, he would bring that woman with him again. They would sun themselves out on the bank, but he still slept with one eye open, keeping a watch on her.

Then they would go back again. This went on for a long time. Finally, they went out one day. That old crocodile stretched out in the sand, sunning himself, sunning himself. The sun got hotter and hotter.

The woman looked at that crocodile and said, 'Oh, he's really asleep all right. This time he's really sleeping.'

She stood up slowly, didn't make a noise. She walked over near him and picked up a stick. She held it out and snapped it in two. Crrraaack! That old crodocile never woke up; he just kept snoring, fast asleep.

The woman moved over very quietly and then she put on some speed and began to run. Suddenly that old crocodile woke

up with a start and saw his wife running away. He jumped up and began to run after her. She ran as fast as she could, and he was chasing behind her, chasing behind her . . . .

Pretty soon she came close to the camp where all the people were. The people saw her and began to point and shout: 'There, look over there! See that woman running!' The men hurriedly grabbed their spears and sticks and everything, getting ready for that crocodile to come. They wanted to spear him or club him when he came close.

When the woman got close to the camp, the people all ran up to meet her and catch her so she wouldn't be frightened any more. And they waited to see that crocodile coming so they could spear him and kill him.

But the cunning old Ganhaarr never came.

After a time, the men went out to try and hunt him down, and they found something very strange. All along the path where that woman had run, in her fright, they found crocodile eggs, where that lady had dropped them. She had been that old crocodile's wife for so long that she had started to lay crocodile eggs!

But what became of that old crocodile, or that woman's little baby, no one knows to this day.

The giant Dindurr eel

There used to be a big camp near the Endeavour River, and all kinds of people lived there. The two Frill Lizard brothers camped there, too.

Now these two Frill Lizard brothers boasted a lot. They said they could do this, and they could do that. 'Nobody can kill us; nobody can spear us', they would say. 'And we're very good with spears ourselves. We can kill anybody we please.'

All the other people in the camp feared these two brothers.

One day everybody in camp went down to the river. The tide was coming in, and they all wanted to catch crabs and spear fish. They were gathering crabs and spearing stingarees and other river fish when someone saw great ripples coming up the river.

'Hey,' someone cried, 'look down there! Here comes a giant yiirmbal, a gigantic spirit creature! It looks like a huge eel coming under water!'

And it was a monstrous eel. We call it a dindurr.

All the rest of those people were frightened of the giant eel, and they moved away from the bank of the river. But those two Frill Lizard brothers, who were always boasting and calling themselves brave, weren't afraid. They stood near the bank, and hooked their spears in their spear-throwers.

'We two will spear that yiirmbal by and by,' they said. 'Let him come!'

The huge eel came up up the river, closer and closer. When he came right to where those two brothers were standing, they put both their spears right into him.

The eel rolled over, twisting this way and that, from the pain of those two spears. He rolled and rolled, and broke the two spears off.

The two Frill Lizard brothers didn't know which way to run. They jumped up and headed straight for the mountain called Bilbiirr. They thought they might hide in a cave on the mountain side.

That giant eel began to follow them. He couldn't chase them above the ground, so he went underground, moving fast. As the two brothers went for that mountain, the big eel came after them. When he got close, he opened his huge mouth wide, and rose up out of the ground to swallow them up.

But the two brothers were just in front of him, and they kept on running.

He came up behind them again. He opened his mouth and pushed up through the ground to eat them. But they were just too fast for him, and they got away again.

But the eel kept after them, travelling fast underground. He was right on their heels, and for the third time, he opened his mouth wide open, and made a grab for them, coming up through the ground right behind them. But again they were running too quickly, and they ran right up the mountain side and hid in a cave.

Well, that big dindurr came up and began to search all around, looking for those two Frill Lizard brothers. He cast his eyes all around, and he caught sight of old Dharramali, the Thunder Storm. Since he couldn't see where those two Frill Lizards had gone, he went up to old Storm and told him what had happened.

Old Storm was a bit startled when he heard the story, and he ran off to pick up some thunderbolts. But he was in a hurry and he only took two thunderbolts along. He looked around and saw the cave in the mountain side. He took those thunderbolts and he struck that cave with lightning: crash! first on one side. And then: crash! on the other side.

But those two Frill Lizard brothers hid right up in the far corner of the cave, where the lightning bolts couldn't reach them. That's how the two Frill Lizard brothers were saved.

But that mountain, Bilbiirr, still has the marks where old Storm struck it with lightning. And in the three places where that giant eel rose up to try and catch the Frill Lizard brothers, today you can see three big waterholes that never dry up.

14

How the giant Nhinhinhi fish changed the languages

Long ago all men had a single language, which everyone could understand.

One time word went out to all the different tribes of people that there would be a big dance. People came together from the East, from the West, from the North and from the South. They all gathered together at a big lagoon called Ngurrayin, to have their corroboree.

They used to go out hunting of a daytime. Some would spear game for meat. Others might go after bush tucker, look for yams and other things. Still others would chop down trees and get the honey in them.

In the evening they would all come back to that big lagoon. They used to cook the meat and yams, and then everybody would have a big feed. They would sit down and eat and eat and eat.

When everyone was full, they would get up, and start the dance.

This went on night after night, for some time.

Now this place, Ngurrayin, is a big lagoon. In the summertime, no matter how hot it is, that water never dries up. It is fresh water, but the old people say that sea water comes underground from the ocean and holds the water in that lagoon up. That's why it never dries up, you see, because it is connected to the sea underground.

Well, there was a giant fish, a nhinhinhi or groper, that came up from the sea, from the East. It came along underground towards the lagoon where all those different tribes were having their dance. When it got there it opened up its gigantic mouth, and it rose up out of the water, and swallowed the whole jolly lot of them.

Then that giant fish turned around and headed East again, travelling underground until it reached the sea.

For two months that groper stayed in the sea, with all the people inside of him. Then he came again from the East, just the same way, travelling underground. When he got to the lagoon he opened up his mouth and vomited all the people out again.

The people jumped down onto the ground and they began walking all about. But when they tried to speak to one another, they found that they were all speaking different languages. One man would talk one way, and another man would talk another way. And the first one couldn't understand the other one.

Well that's why Aboriginal people talk different languages until today.

The two night owl sisters and their Leichhardt tree

There were once two night owl sisters. They owned a big Leichhardt tree, which they called by the name of Dyilbi. This was the only tree of its kind anywhere in the world, and it used to bear fruit all the year round. The two night owl sisters would gather Leichhardt fruit from one month to another, and they used to have good feeds on all that fruit.

Those Bunydya sisters are known as night owls because they move about at night. They used to eat their Leichhardt fruit in the night time, and then go back and sleep all day.

Well, in time a white cockatoo named Waandaar began to come around during the day, when those two sisters were sleeping. He used to sneak around and steal the fruit from off

the Dyilbi tree. He would steal and steal and steal. Then he would take all the fruit he could carry away to a tall tea-tree and eat it.

In the evening the Bunydya sisters woke up from sleep. As night fell they would come over to their Leichhardt tree and look for fruit. They searched and searched and searched. No fruit. All the ripe ones had been eaten up.

'Say, who has been stealing our Dyilbi fruit and eating it?' they asked each other.

After this happened for some time, the two sisters called Frill Lizard over to their camp. This is what they said to him: 'If you want to marry us, to make us your wives, then you should go and watch to see who is stealing our Dyilbi fruit.'

Well, old Frill Lizard had fallen in love with those night owl sisters, so when they went to sleep the next day, he went and hid by a tree. And there he waited, watching the Leichhardt tree and keeping a lookout.

By and by that White Cockatoo came sneaking up. He looked all around, this way and that, but he couldn't see anybody. Then he began to pick fruit from the Dyilbi tree. When he had picked all the ripe ones, he gathered them up, and took them away to eat.

Old Frill Lizard waited until the White Cockatoo had gone, and then when night fell he went to tell the Night Owl sisters what he had seen. 'It's that old White Cockatoo who is eating your fruit,' he said.

'Hmmm,' said the Bunydya sisters. 'Well, if you want to marry us then you must go and find out where Waandaar camps. And then you must kill him.'

Frill Lizard went back and made a spear and a spear-thrower. He hid again near the Leichhardt tree, waiting to spear that Cockatoo when he came to steal the fruit. He had painted himself all up with clay so that Cockatoo wouldn't smell him.

But that old Waandaar had sharp eyes, too. When he came near, he saw Frill Lizard behind the tree, and he flew away. Old Frill Lizard didn't know how to catch him, but he ran as fast as he could, following White Cockatoo. That's how he learned that Waandaar was camping in a tea-tree.

Well, Frill Lizard waited until the sun set in the West. As night fell, that White Cockatoo settled down to sleep high up on the tea-tree. Frill Lizard got his firesticks, made from the Bulal tree, and ran up to the trunk of the tree where Waandaar was sleeping.

Then Frill Lizard sat down and began to rub his firesticks together. He rubbed and he rubbed, and pretty soon a glowing spark fell onto the bark and sticks he had put down. He blew on the spark, until the tea-tree bark caught fire.

Very quickly the flames ran up the tree, burning the bark and branches, and giving off a cloud of black smoke. The fire reached that old White Cockatoo so quickly that it turned him entirely black.

That is how Nguurraarr the Black Cockatoo was made. Before there were only white cockatoos, until one was turned black by the smoke of that fire.

And now there are Leichhardt trees all over the place, too, since Cockatoo used to steal that fruit and drop the seeds all over. Before there was only that one tree that belonged to the Bunydya sisters.

The old woman and her grandson on a lonely island

Once there was an old woman, who lived with her grandson on a lonely island in the East. It was just a small island, and those two were the only ones who lived there. They were all alone.

That old woman used to get hungry for meat. So she would send her grandson out hunting, for fish.

The boy would take his spear and his milbiir, his spear-thrower, and set out to spear fish. He would walk right around the island hunting. In the evening he would bring home what he had caught. Sometimes he would bring home a gundirru, a big brown stingray. Sometimes he might spear a spotted one, called yidi. Sometimes he would bring home yalnganydyi, a crescent-shaped stingray. But all he ever brought home was stingray, sometimes three or four at once.

One night the old grandmother got very sick from eating all those stingrays every day. In the morning she was still sick, and she got very angry with that little boy.

She called the little boy over, and she began to blow in his ear. She made him forget about everything and do just what she said. And she put a curse on him: 'From now on,' she said, 'you have to travel just one path. You have to start in the East and go towards the West, all your life. And as you grow up, you won't grow straight. Instead you'll have to bend around, and grow crooked and round just like all those stingrays that you speared.'

She changed that little boy into a Moon. We still see that Moon travelling from East to West. And as it grows it bends around just like a stingray. That little boy is still under his grandmother's spell.

The forest spirit and his ten beautiful daughters

Diimuur, the forest spirit, had ten daughters. They were all very beautiful, with long long hair. They lived together in a cave high on a mountainside. Nearby was a waterfall where they often went to swim.

This Diimuur was a great giant of a man, whose face was covered with a thick beard. He was also very fierce. Everyone was afraid of this old forest spirit.

In his cave, the old fellow kept all kinds of spears, and boomerangs, and spear-throwers, and clubs, and other sorts of weapon.

Where the river flowed down from the mountains there was another camp where people lived. One person who lived there was Gabul, the Carpet Snake. He, too, was very brave, a good hunter, and a great fighter.

One day, Carpet Snake had an idea. He said to all the others in the camp, 'I'm going to go up on the mountain side and see that Old Man Diimuur.'

'Go on, then,' said the others.

So Gabul, the Carpet Snake, got himself ready. First he went down to the river to have a swim. When he had washed himself all over, he went looking around for some soft clay. He painted himself all over with the clay, just to protect himself in case that Diimuur might smell him. Then he set off up the mountain.

He climbed and he climbed and he climbed. He went higher and higher up the side of the mountain, until he came to that cave.

He went inside very softly and looked around. He saw the spears, and he saw the spear-throwers. He saw the boomerangs, and he saw the clubs. But that old forest spirit himself was not in the cave.

So old Gabul turned around and went outside again. 'Where could they all be?' he asked himself.

He headed down towards the waterfall to spy them out. He peeped around silently, and soon he caught sight of old Diimuur sitting on a rock near the water. His many daughters were there, too, with their long, long hair.

Well, old Carpet Snake dropped down and started to crawl. He crawled along, very quiet, until he had come up close behind the old fellow. Suddenly he jumped up and grabbed old Diimuur and threw him to the ground.

They both thrashed around, grabbing each other. That old forest spirit rolled and thrashed about, trying to break loose. But Carpet Snake held him still more tightly, and wouldn't let him go. No matter how hard old Diimuur wrestled, he couldn't get away.

Finally, as Carpet Snake held him to the ground, that old spirit sang out: 'Let me go, let me go! Let me loose!'

'I won't let you loose,' said Gabul, 'unless you promise to give me one of your daughters to marry.'

'All right,' that old fellow said, 'you can take one.'

Carpet Snake let go of that old spirit then. He got up and went over to look at the ten beautiful daughters. He looked at each one, and he found one that was the most beautiful of all. That was the daughter that he took away with him.

He brought her with him back down to the camp at the foot of the mountain.

All the others saw Carpet Snake coming back to camp, with his new wife following behind him. They saw that the new wife was very, very beautiful. And they all felt very jealous of old Gabul, because of his new wife.

The two of them came into camp and went into Carpet Snake's house. They stayed there together for three days and three nights. But in that time Carpet Snake's new wife would eat no food, and she would drink no water.

Carpet Snake began to feel worried. He said to himself, 'My wife might die, if she doesn't eat.'

So he got up, early in the morning when the dew was still on the ground, and he took his new wife down to the river, to try and cheer her up.

But when they came near to the river, that old forest spirit's daughter jumped straight into the water. Once she was under water she changed into a fish, and began to swim up the river, towards the waterfall. She swam and she swam and she swam, and at last she came back to her father high in the mountains.

Meanwhile, poor old Gabul waited and waited and waited. 'When is my wife going to come up out of the water again?' he thought.

He waited a while longer, and then he got angry and left the place. He headed back to the camp to tell the others what had happened.

As he came close to the camp, old Kookaburra caught sight of him coming back without his wife. He began to laugh at that Carpet Snake.

Carpet Snake told the others the story: how his wife had jumped in the water and not come up. But they all crowded around and began to laugh and laugh and laugh.

Old Carpet Snake felt ashamed, and he crawled off, out of the camp.

Well, today, when we see old Carpet Snake crawling around, he always moves very slowly. He still has a broken heart, because his beautiful wife left him.

Frill Lizard and the honey

Frill Lizard had two sisters, two blackbirds. One day he decided to go out hunting, and he called his sisters to come along with him.

They set out and walked and walked. Frill Lizard happened to look up in a tree, as they were walking. There he spied a bees' nest.

He said to his sisters, 'Did you see, up in the tree, where that honey is? You two wait down here, and I'll climb up and get it.'

Frill Lizard got his stone axe, and he started to climb. He used the axe to chop notches in the tree, and he climbed up and up until he reached the branch where the honey was. Then he began to chop at the branch. Soon he had chopped an opening in the wood just big enough for him to get his hand in.

He reached in through the hole and took a handful of honey. He pulled it out and ate that first lot all by himself.

He put his hand in a second time, and he was about to eat it when those two sisters sang out from down below: 'Hey, you, throw some of that honey down to us. Throw some to us!'

Frill Lizard called back, 'Wait a bit, wait a bit!'

Then he put his hand in the hole and brought out another handful of honey.

'Here, here, I'll throw it down to you,' he cried.

Those two sisters stretched out their hands to catch that honey as it came down. But just at the last minute, instead of throwing the honey down, Frill Lizard went Whooomp! and threw the honey right up into his own mouth. He ate it himself.

His sisters kept singing out for him to throw some of the honey down to them. So he put his hand in the hole again, and drew out another handful.

'Now watch out, get ready, I'm going to throw this lot down,' he shouted.

Those two sisters started to feel very greedy, now, and they stretched their hands up again to catch the honey.

But once again, Frill Lizard went Whooomp! and put the honey in his own mouth.

'Well,' Frill Lizard sang out, 'I can't throw the honey down just like that. You two have to go look around for some baaydjin grass. I'll make a sponge and dip it in the honey. Then I can throw that down for you to suck the honey from.'

So the two sisters went to have a look around. They searched and they searched, but they couldn't find any baaydjin grass.

They came back and they called up to their brother, 'No baaydjin grass around here!'

Frill Lizard said, 'Never mind. One of you take off that little skirt you're wearing and throw that up. I'll dip that in the honey.'

So one of the blackbird sisters untied the little yirrbi she had around her waist, and she threw it high up to her brother in the tree.

Frill Lizard took that yirrbi and stuck it in the opening. He dipped in the honey and sopped it up until it was full. Then he pulled it out. But instead of throwing the skirt, soaked with honey, down to his sisters, Frill Lizard sucked that honey out himself. And he was so greedy that he swallowed the whole thing, skirt and all.

Well, his sister's skirt got stuck in Frill Lizard's throat. And from that time on, when Frill Lizard gets excited he grows a lump on his throat. Well, that lump is his sister's yirrbi, which he wasn't even supposed to touch, and which he sucked honey from.

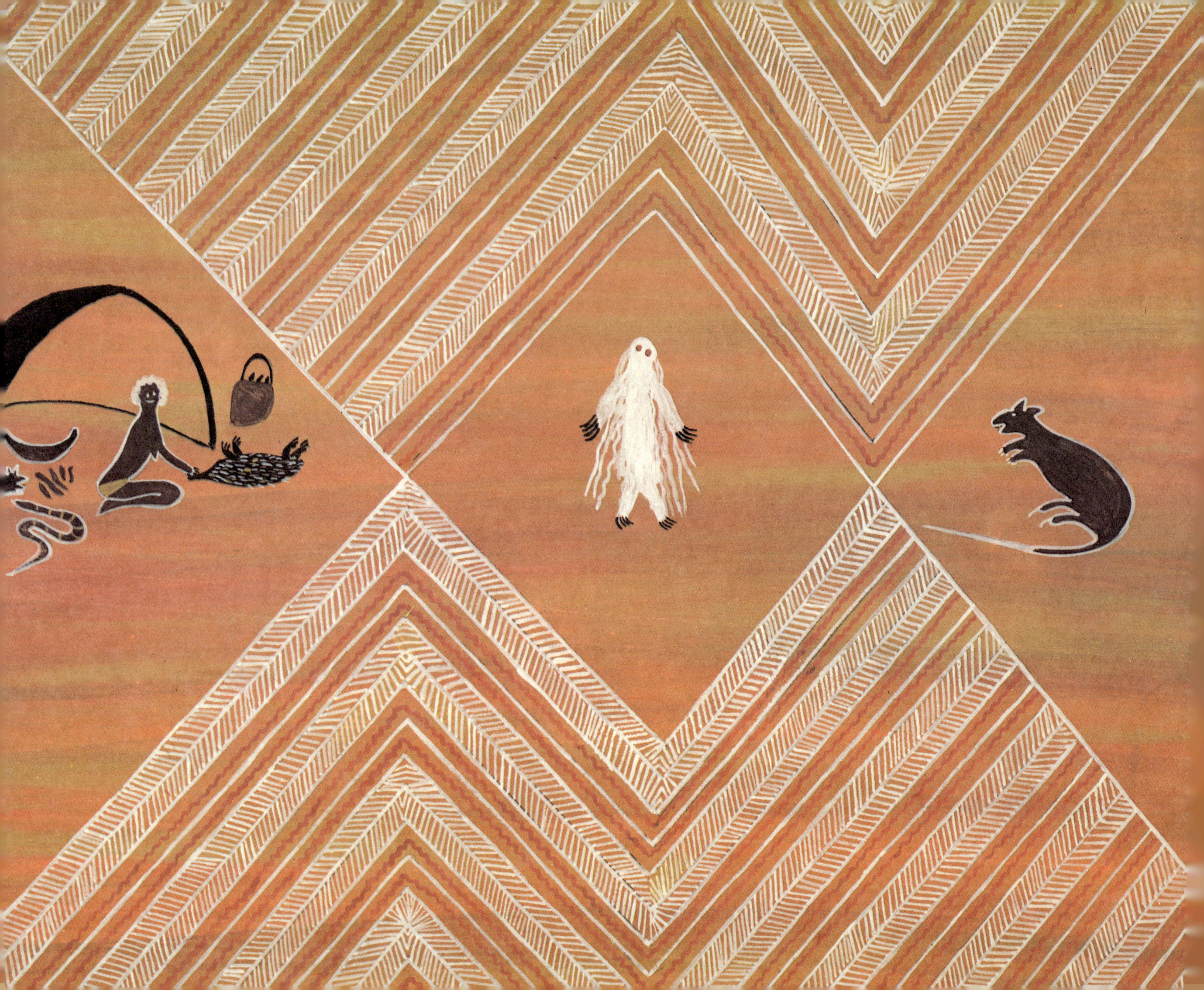

Durrgin, the water rat

In the early days, when a person got too old to hunt or to travel, the other people in the tribe would make a final camp for him and leave him to die.

Well, that happened to one old woman. She had grown too old. She couldn't walk around any more, and she couldn't gather food. So the rest of the tribe decided to leave her.

All the people went out and they gathered different kinds of food. They got different kinds of mayi or bush tucker: they got yellow yams, and white yams. They got honey. They killed meat: wallaby and porcupine. They heaped all the food up for the old lady, and they said to her, 'You go on and eat all this food, now. We're going to leave you here.' And they left her sitting down with all that food.

After they had shifted camp, the old woman found herself all alone. After some days, when she had eaten all the food and meat, she lay down, ready to die.

Now there was a kind of spirit or ghost, called a Wudhi, who was travelling around all over the country. He happened to come upon that camp where the old woman had been left.

The Wudhi saw the old woman lying there and he came up to her. 'What are you doing here all by yourself?' he asked her.

'Oh, the rest of them left me here to die,' said the old woman.

'No, you don't want to stay by yourself like that. What do you want to die for?' said that spirit. 'I'll go find a bees' nest, and chop some honey for you.'

He went out looking around for honey. Soon he found a bees' nest. He chopped it down and put all the honey in a piece of tea-tree bark. Then he carried it back to the old woman's camp.

The old woman was very happy to see that Wudhi coming back, because she thought she was going to get a bit of a feed on that honey.

The spirit came up and sat down. But he was a good way away from where the old woman was sitting.

He said, 'Are you feeling hungry?'

'Yes,' she told him, 'I'm hungry. Come on, now, give me some of that honey to eat.' And she stretched out her hand to take it.

The spirit grabbed some honey in his hand and held it out to the old woman. 'Here, here,' he said, 'take this, take this . . . .'

But just as that old woman reached out to take the honey, the spirit went Whooomp! and gobbled it down himself.

Once again, the Wudhi took some honey and held it out to her. But every time that old woman tried to take the honey from him, the spirit would go Whooomp! and eat it himself.

After two or three times, the woman began to get wild with anger. She picked up a big yamstick that was lying nearby, and she started to hit that spirit. She hit him, and hit him, and each time she hit him he backed away a little further, a little further . . . and suddenly he jumped up and ran off. She chased that spirit away.

Well, the Wudhi ran and ran until he came to a place where there was a high waterfall. He thought, 'Ahh, this is a good place for me to camp.' So he stopped there and he made his camp.

He went out the next day and gathered a big heap of badhuurr nuts from the zamia palm. He brought them home and cooked them in an earth oven. Then he pounded the nuts, and set them in the creek for a few days, to wash all the poison out of them. After they were ready, he made those nuts into a kind of cake. And he had stacks of those cakes, all around his camp.

He had a good feed, and, feeling quite satisfied, he lay down to sleep.

But the spirit didn't know that in the river there by the waterfall lived Durrgin, the water rat.

When the spirit was fast asleep, the water rat came up out of the water. He found those zamia palm cakes, and he started to eat them. He ate and ate and ate, until dawn. Then, still early in the morning, he jumped back in the water.

Old Wudhi woke up from sleep. He saw right away that some of his badhuurr cakes were missing. 'Now, who has been eating my mayi?' he said.

He started looking around for footprints or tracks. He walked all around the camp, and went right up to the riverbank. But there were no tracks to be seen.

Well, the spirit said to himself: 'Somebody's been stealing my food at night. Tonight I won't go to sleep. I'll keep my eyes open and see who the thief is.'

That night, when the sun went down, the spirit didn't build a fire. He stayed awake, sitting in the darkness. He waited and he waited and he waited.

Just as it was beginning to get very late, the spirit saw old Durrgin the water rat coming up out of the water. Durrgin sat down and began to eat the cakes.

Old Wudhi saw the water rat, and very quietly he picked up his spear and his spear-thrower. He hooked the spear up, and Whooosh! he let it fly.

But old Durrgin jumped to one side just in time. The spear missed.

Then Durrgin grabbed up one last badhuurr cake, and he was off. He ran straight up on top of the ridge of the mountain right there. The spirit picked up all his spears, and chased after him.

Well, that Durrgin jumped from the first mountain, Bald Hill, right over to the next mountain, Mt Harris, which we call Nugal Dyin.gurr. He kept running right along the ridge, but that spirit was right behind him.

From there, old Durrgin jumped over to a little hill called Gugaabarr. Old Wudhi was still chasing him.

Finally that water rat made for the mountain called Indian Head. He found a cave there, and he ran inside, right to the deepest part.

The spirit came up, and looked around for him. He looked all around but he couldn't see that water rat. And that's how old Durrgin escaped.

Well, the mountain where the water rat hid is still called Durrginbigu, which means 'where the Durrgin is'. That is the name of the cave, right on the point.

And today you can still see the waterfall where the old spirit made his camp. There are big square rocks heaped all around that place, just like the zamia palm cakes that old Wudhi made.

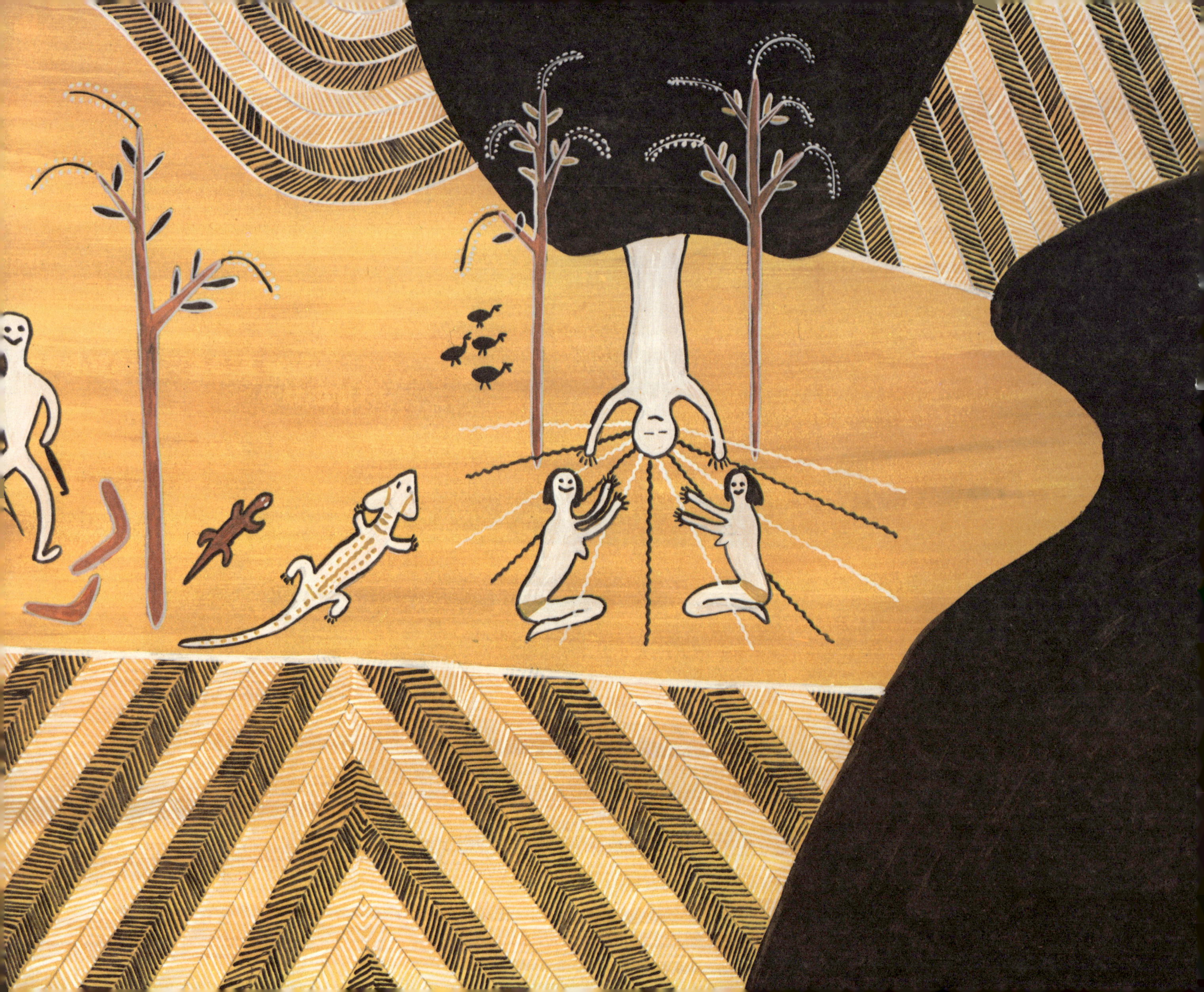

Fog and Thunderstorm

Old man Fog lived in the North. He belonged to an area called Yidamugu. Thunderstorm lived in the South. He came from the area called Muunhdhi. Now, Thunderstorm married old Fog's twin daughters, and he took them away to live with him in the South.

One day, Thunderstorm went out hunting. He called his two wives to come along with him. They walked and walked, through the bush, looking for yams and honey, looking for edible roots, and trying to kill some meat.

After a while they came to a big swamp. There were lots of water lilies floating in it.

Thunderstorm said to his wives, 'You two dive around here in this waterhole. Maybe you can find us some lily roots to eat. As for me, I'll just have a walk around the place to see what I can find.'

So he left the two women at the swamp, and he set out again through the bush. Pretty soon he came upon some vines from yam plants. There were lots of yams around there. But they all belonged to Thunderstorm's father-in-law, Fog.

Well, there was nobody around, so Thunderstorm got a sharp yam stick, and he started to dig. He dug and dug, and helped himself to the yams that he found. He took his dilly bag and filled it right up with the yams.

Then he got up and went back to the swamp. He picked up his wives again, and they all went home to their camp.

Well, while this was going on, old Fog had been lying down asleep. While Thunderstorm was digging the yams, a big wind came up. The wind picked up a leaf from one of the yams. It blew that leaf, and blew it, right up North until it landed on old Fog's face, where he slept. It woke him up.

Old Fog sat up out of a sound sleep, opened his eyes, and picked up the leaf. He had a good look at it. He said to himself, 'This leaf is from *my* yams, and somebody is digging them up.'

Old Fog began to feel very angry, that someone would steal his yams. He wanted to find out who the culprit was. So he got up and took his boomerang. He threw it off to the East, but pretty soon that boomerang came back again. Then he threw the boomerang off to the North, but it came back again. Then he threw it off to the West, but it wasn't long before that boomerang came back again. Finally, old Fog threw the boomerang off to the South. This time, the boomerang didn't come back again.

'Oh,' said Fog, 'so it's my son-in-law Thunderstorm who has been stealing my yams. Well, I'm going to go spear him now.'

All right, Fog went looking around for a strong tree to make a spear from. He cut down one tree and made a spear. But when he tried throwing it, he found it was no good. He tried another kind of tree, but the spear was no good. He made a third spear, a fourth . . . but all the spears were no good. Finally Fog went out to the sandhill, and there he cut down a Mirrbi tree. He took it back to his camp, and he made a spear from it. He took that spear, and to try it out he speared a large tree near his camp.

The spear made from the Mirrbi tree was so strong that it went clear through the first tree and speared the next tree behind it, too.

'This spear will do,' thought Fog, as he pulled it out. 'This is the one I'll use to spear my thieving son-in-law.'

Next Fog called Bunydyul the Frill Lizard to his camp, and he told him what to do. 'I want you to go South,' he said, 'and find out where that old Thunderstorm is, and what he's doing. I want to spear him.'

So Frill Lizard set out, and he travelled South. He went and he went until he came close to Thunderstorm's camp. He could hear the sound of Thunderstorm snoring. Quickly he looked around for the tallest tree, and climbed up to the top. He peered around and saw Thunderstorm fast asleep. His head was sitting right on the ground, and his feet were high up in the clouds. He was sleeping between two trees. His two wives sat on either side of him, cleaning and combing out his hair.

'Hmmm,' said Frill Lizard to himself. He jumped down from that tree and ran, as fast as he could go, back to old Fog's camp. He told old Fog that he had seen Thunderstorm, and that he was asleep.

All right, Fog got his spear made from the Mirrbi tree, and his spear-thrower. He went down to the river and had a swim to wash himself. Then he smeared himself all over with clay, so that his son-in-law wouldn't be able to smell him.

Then he picked up his weapons and headed South. He walked along until he came close to Thunderstorm's camp. Then he fell down on all fours and began to crawl closer and closer. As he was sneaking up, the little birds began to chatter and laugh at him.

Thunderstorm opened his eyes and said to one of his wives, 'You go and have a look at what those little birds are laughing at. There might be a carpet snake or something we can kill and eat.'

One of the women got up, and went over to where the birds were laughing. There she saw her old father, Fog.

Fog said to his daughter, 'Don't tell your husband I'm here.

Don't say anything. But you and your sister keep clear, because I'm going to spear that Thunderstorm.'

So the woman went back to her husband. Thunderstorm asked her what the birds were laughing at.

'Nothing,' she said. 'There's nothing there, not even a carpet snake.'

'Hmmm,' said Thunderstorm.

The wife sat down, and she whispered to her sister to stand clear.

Meanwhile, old Fog sneaked closer and closer. When he came up close, he hurled his spear. That spear travelled right through one tree on the Eastern side. Then it pierced Thunderstorm through and went right on through the tree on the Western side.

There was old Thunderstorm hung up in the middle. He started to spin, over and over; he didn't know what to do. And he started throwing out his thunderbolts, trying to strike Fog, and howling with pain. The old people say, when we hear Dharramali, the Thunderstorm, rumbling in the distance, that he is howling with pain from being speared.

Well, Thunderstorm kept throwing his lightning bolts at old Fog. But Fog ducked down lower and lower, and finally he buried himself right in the ground. Then he began to travel underground, to get away from his angry son-in-law. He travelled and didn't come up again until he was high on the mountain side, near a cave.

Before he went into the cave, Fog picked up a little red lizard, called Gunhdhirr. He blew in his ear, and blew and blew, saying, 'Shooo, turn into a little boy!' Pretty soon that magic spell took effect, and the lizard became a little boy. Then the two of them hurried into the cave, and hid there.

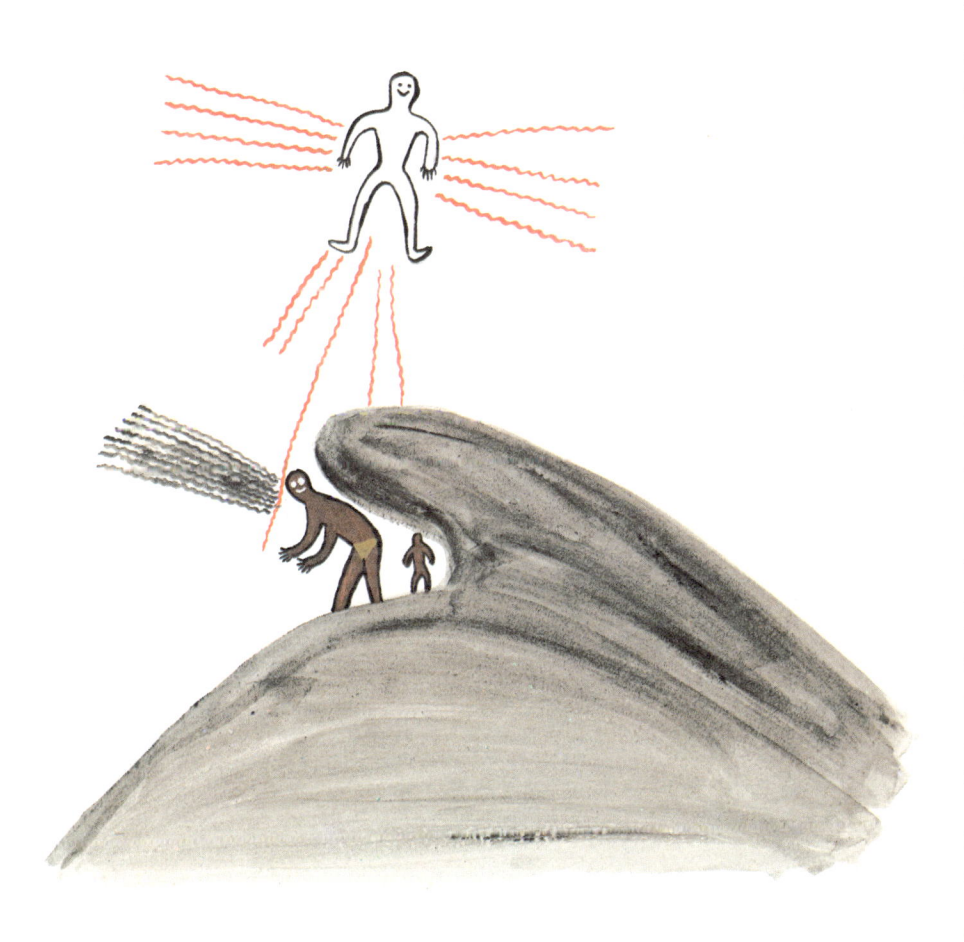

They camped there all night long. Fog knew that Thunderstorm was circling overhead, waiting to strike them with lightning.

The next morning, the little boy got up and said, 'Father, I want to go outside.'

Fog said, 'No, no. You can't go outside. Thunderstorm is waiting out there to strike us with lightning.'

After a little while the little boy asked again, 'Can I go outside?'

'No, no,' said Fog. 'Thunderstorm will strike you. I told you that before.'

But the little boy kept pestering old Fog. 'I want to go outside to have a look around.'

Finally Fog said, 'All right, you wait here. I'll go outside and have a look to see where Thunderstorm is.'

But Thunderstorm was waiting for him. As soon as old Fog poked his head outside the cave, Storm threw a lightning bolt. Before Fog could duck down out of the way, the lightning blew his beard right off.

Today, when we see clouds floating over the mountains, the old people say that they are really the beard of old Wurrbal, the Fog.

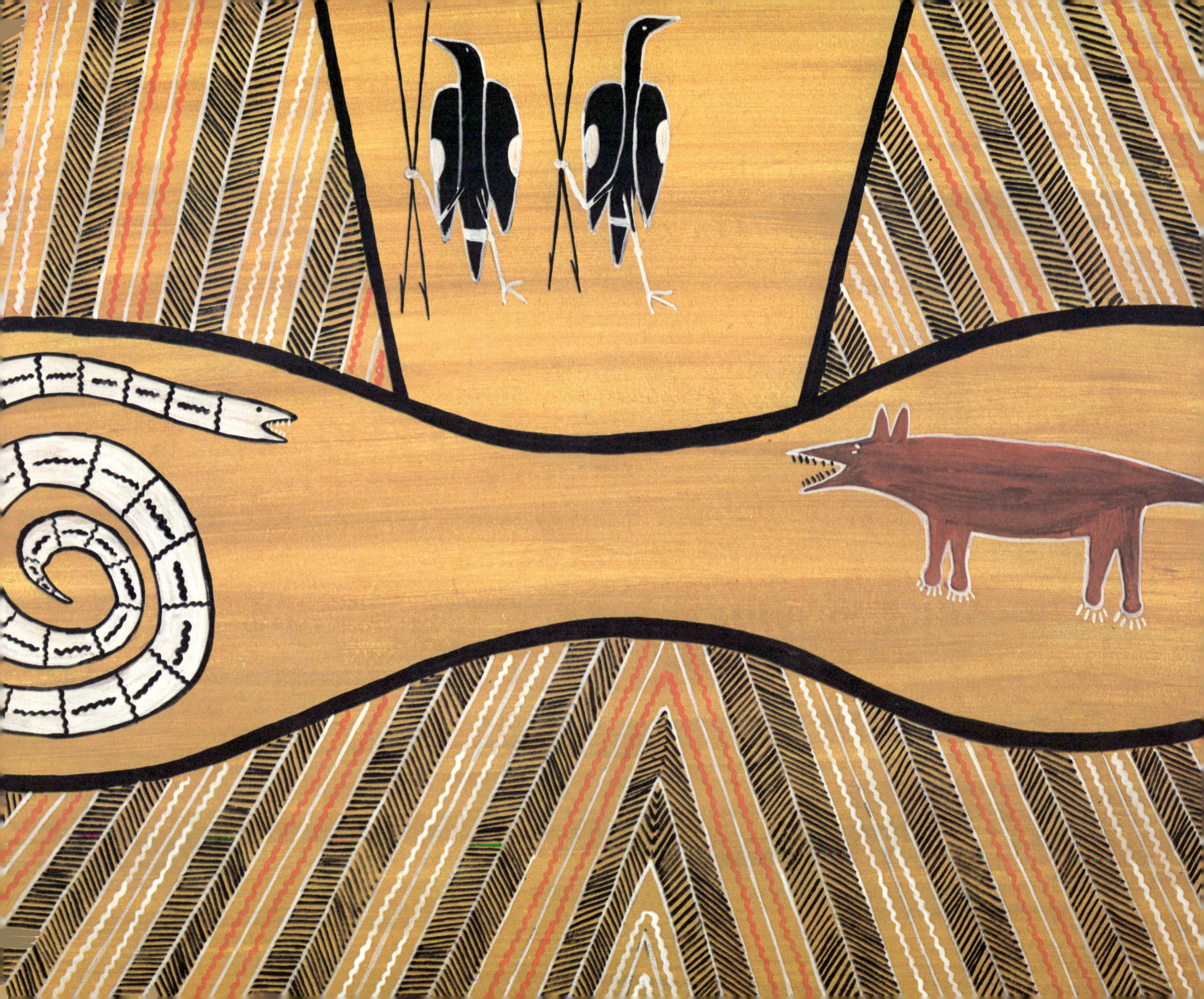

The giant dingo dog

There were two magpie brothers, who lived in their own camp. They were not only very great hunters, but they wanted all creatures to live in peace. They used to go out from camp to camp, visiting people, to see if they were living peacefully. If they found people fighting, or hunting each other and making trouble, or if they saw people angry and hateful towards one another, they would spear them. They would try to put them off the road they were following. Any wild men or women or fierce animals that they met they would kill, if they wouldn't behave themselves.

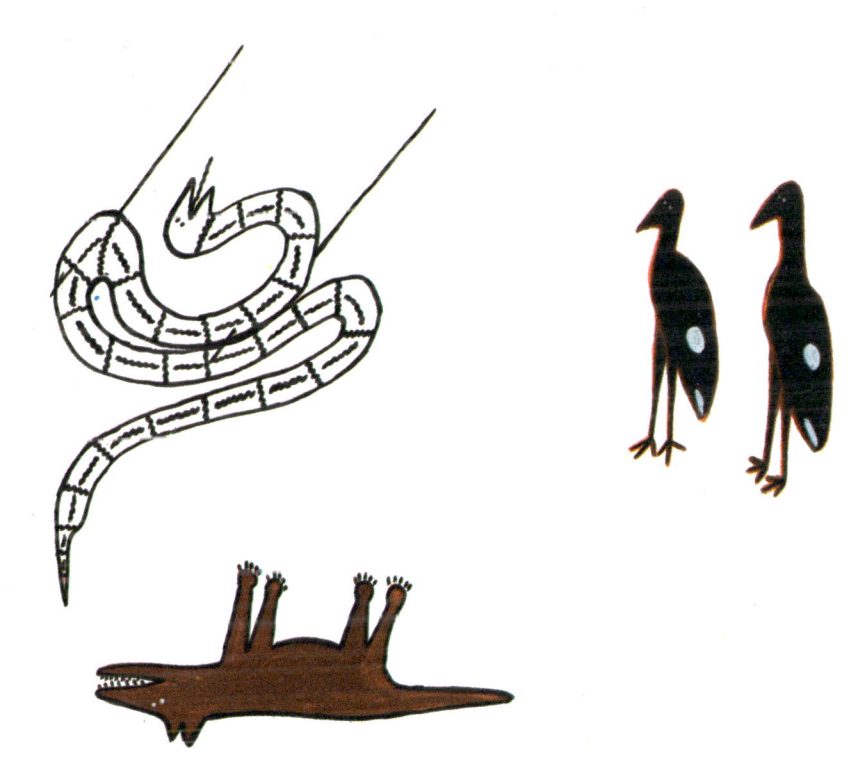

This went on for a good while.

Now there was an old carpet snake who didn't like this idea. He had a gigantic dog, a huge dingo. He decided to send his dog out to hunt those two magpie brothers, to make them stop what they were doing. So he sent him out to find the two brothers. For several days he tried to find them without any luck.

Meanwhile, those two magpie brothers came to hear about the carpet snake sending his giant dog out after them. They decided to spear the dog, so they each sat down and made two Murranggal spears.

Then they got up and went to the river to have a swim. They painted themselves all over with clay, and they went up on a high mountain to have a look around. They looked in all directions, East, West, North and South, trying to catch sight of that giant dingo.

They waited for a long time, looking all around. Late in the afternoon, as the sun was just going down, they saw the dog coming their way. Quickly they ran down to cover the road where he would pass by, one on one side and one on the other.

The giant dog came closer and closer. He was so huge that they could see him walking along with his nose high in the air, trying to sniff them out. But he couldn't smell them because they were all painted with clay.

The two magpie brothers waited until he was right close to them. Then they both stood up at once and threw their spears into him from either side.

That giant dog fell to the ground, and rolled himself over and over with pain. He thrashed about and broke off the spears. Then he picked himself up, and ran straight back to his master, the old carpet snake.

As the dog came into camp, that old carpet snake saw him, and he said to himself, 'What? Have they speared my dog?' Suddenly he himself began to feel very frightened. 'Now those two magpie brothers will be after me to spear me,' he thought.

It was already night time, and that old carpet snake built himself a fire. But instead of sitting down next to the fire, he went into the darkness and sat down, trying to hide.

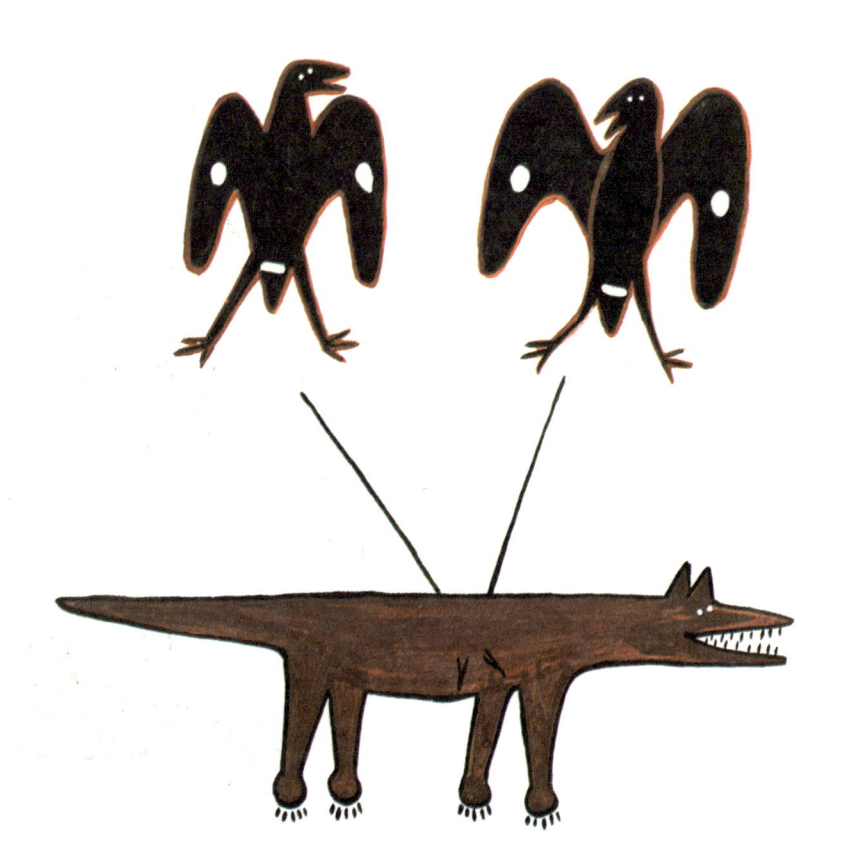

The two magpie brothers had brought their spears and spear-throwers and come looking for that carpet snake. When it got dark, they started to sneak up to his camp. When they came close enough to see, they looked around.

'Where is that carpet snake? He's not by the fire,' said one magpie.

They looked around carefully and by and by they spied that old snake lying in the darkness. 'There he is, away from the fire', they whispered.

The two magpie brothers quietly circled around behind him, and then together they put two spears right into him.

This time, old carpet snake himself rolled over and over with pain, trying to break off the spears. The two magpie brothers didn't want to kill him, so they ran up and grabbed ahold of him. They pulled out the spears, and they began to blow in his ear. 'From now on,' they said to him, 'you must no longer kill human beings.'

And even now, that old carpet snake is not cheeky like other snakes. He is not poisonous, and he won't bite.

Then the two brothers went up to that giant dog. They held him down and they blew in his ear. They said, 'From now on, you must not kill human beings either. But you must cry and wail all your life, in sorrow for those that you have already killed.'

And even today, when we go out in the bush, we hear that dingo howling and singing out. Well, he's crying for the ones that he killed before.

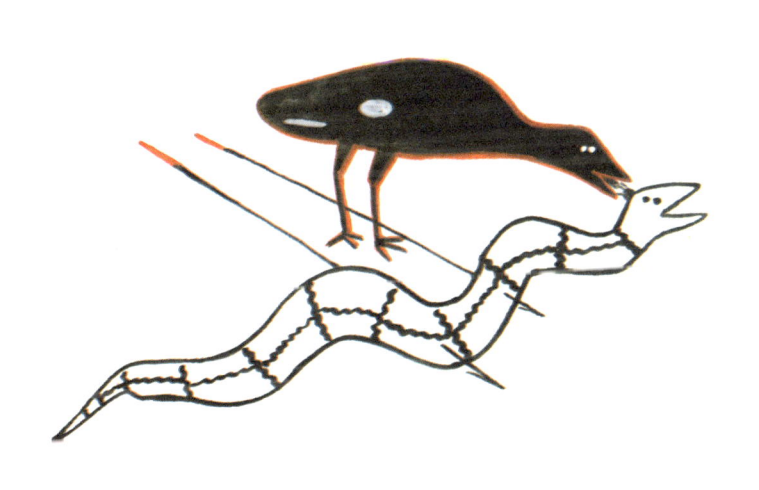

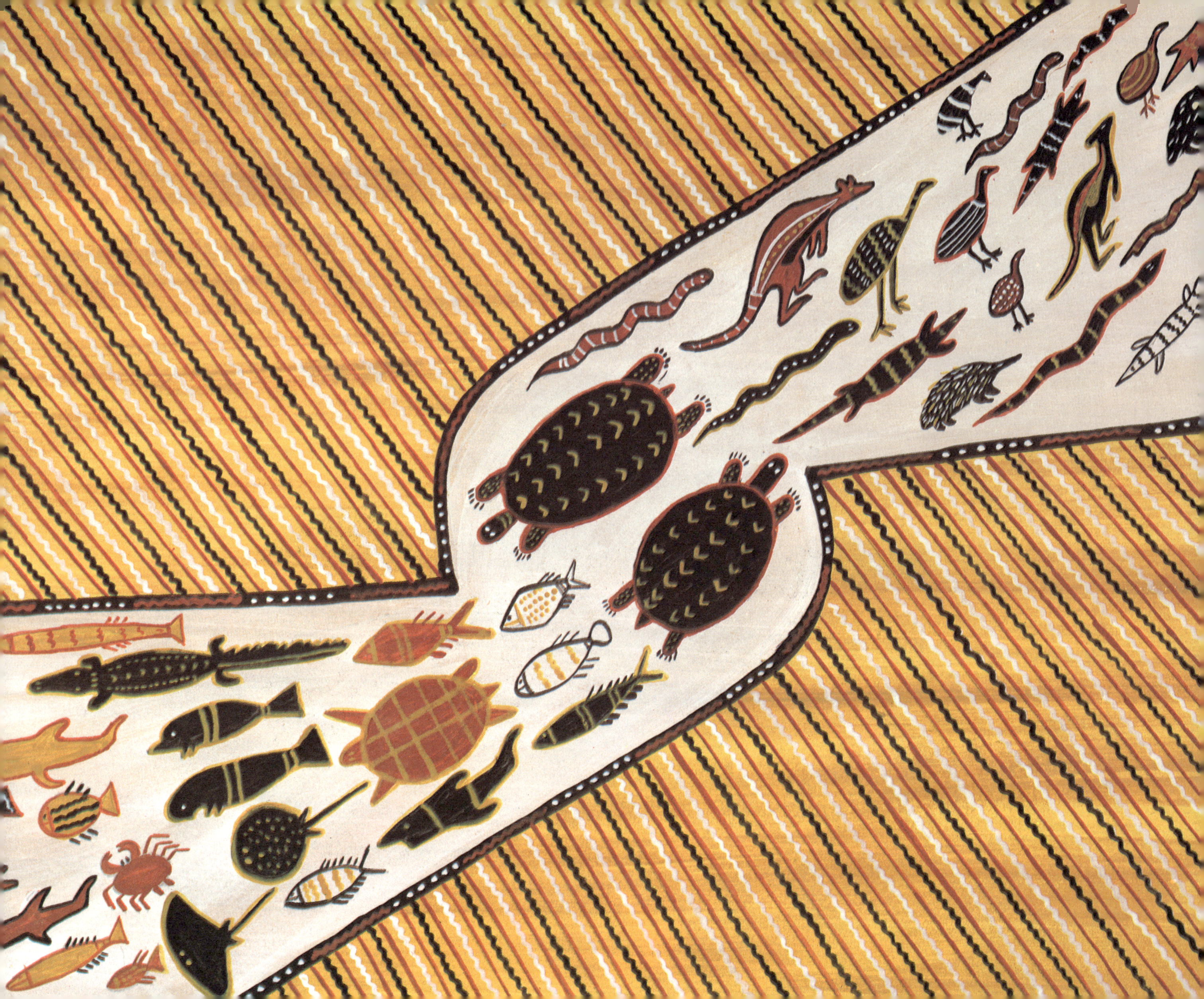

The two Dugul sisters

Once all the creatures, from the land and sea, came together to have a great dance. All the fishes, and sea turtles, and the dugongs, and other creatures of the water assembled for the dance. All the kangaroos, the wallabies, and the emus, and the porcupines, all the lizards and goannas and snakes, and other land creatures also came together.

This was going to be a great corroboree, to last for weeks and even months. But they picked a sandy place to have the dance, a place where there was no water to drink. The name of that place is Wuyii.

When all the creatures had gathered together, they began to dance. For three or four nights they danced and danced. But afterwards they all began to feel very thirsty for a drink of water. They started to hunt around for some fresh water to drink. 'Where can we find water?' they said to each other. But there was none.

Now, the two Dugul sisters, two turtles, were the only ones who didn't join in the search for water. Late in the afternoon, when the dancing was finished, these two turtle sisters would sneak off by themselves and hide. Then they would secretly drink water until their thirsts were quenched, and return to the camp.

The rest of the dancers had only grass and leaves to chew on for a bit of moisture. They were very thirsty indeed.

Another night came, and when the dancing was over, the two turtle sisters again crept off and drank water in secret. This time the rest of the dancers took notice of those Dugul sisters sneaking off after the dance. They started to ask one another, 'Say, do you know where those turtle sisters go after the dance? They seem to be getting water from somewhere.'

'No,' said others, 'we don't know where they go. But they always seem to sneak off and hide over there.'

'Hmmm,' they all said. 'Well, let's get together and pick someone to go and spy on them.'

So they all assembled to decide which creature was the best one to hide and watch what those Dugul sisters did after the dance.

First they said to Sand Goanna, whose name was Dhagay, 'Come on, Dhagay, you go and hide. We'll find out if we can see you.'

So Sand Goanna went off and hid in the undergrowth. Then he sang out, 'Here I am! Can you see me?'

'Yeah, we can see you. Come on back! You're no good.'

Goanna came back, and they sent out Balin-ga the Porcupine to have a try.

From his hiding place he sang out, 'Can you see me?'

'Yes, yes, we see you. Come back. You're no good.'

They asked Bunydyul the Frill Lizard to try. 'Frill Lizard, you go and hide in a tree.'

But they could see Frill Lizard, too. He was no good. Then they sent Carpet Snake to try, and many others. One by one, they all had a go. But none of them was any good. They couldn't hide and they gave themselves away.

48

Finally they asked Walanggar the Death Adder to have a go. 'Go on', they said. 'Go and hide from us.'

'All right,' said Walanggar the Death Adder. 'I'll hide from you.'

Death Adder went off and hid in the sand. When he was well hidden, he sang out, 'Well, can you all see me?'

'No, no, we can't see you. Where are you?'

'I'm here,' he called back. 'Can't you see me?'

Death Adder put up his hand and waved. 'Here, I'm putting up my hand. Can you see me, can you see me?'

'No, no, it's no use. We can't see you. Come on, come on, you're the one! Come back! You're the one to hide!'

Walanggar came back to the others, and they told him what to do.

They said, 'Tonight, before the dance is over, you must get up and leave. Go and hide where those two Dugul sisters can't see you. After the dance they will sneak off to drink water. You must find out how they do it. Hide and watch.'

'All right,' said Death Adder.

That night, before the dance was over, Death Adder got up and left the dance ground to hide. After the dance, when the two turtle sisters crept away to have their drink of water, he was hiding and watching them.

The Dugul sisters first looked all around to see if anyone was watching. They couldn't see anyone. Then they began to poke each other in the chest, until water began to run out. They each drank their fill. All the while Walanggar was watching them. When they had drunk enough, they got up and went back to the dancing ground.

Death Adder waited for them to leave. Then he turned around and went back to the others.

He told them what he had seen. They all gathered around to listen. Then they said, 'All right. Tomorrow we're going to have the biggest dance of all. Now we have to pick which creature is the best and fastest dancer of the lot. Come on, who's going to have a go?'

First, old Burriway the Emu, with his long legs, tried dancing.

He danced around, very fast, but the others said, 'No, no, you're not fast enough.'

Then a big buck kangaroo had a try. He got up and danced around and around, but he was a bit too heavy and slow.

Then Gadaar the Wallaby tried dancing, and Gangurru the Wallaroo tried dancing. Even old Balin.ga the Porcupine had a try. But they were all too slow, or too heavy, or too fat. Each time, the others said, 'No, no, you're too slow. We want to pick the very best dancer, the fastest one of all.'

Last of all, little Dyaydyu the Kangaroo Rat, stood up to dance.

'You have a go,' they said to him.

Little Kangaroo Rat began a shake-a-leg dance, called Yimbaalu. He danced up and down, he danced around and around. The others started clapping and shouting. 'More, more, more!' they yelled. Kangaroo Rat danced around and around, faster and faster, and the others couldn't even see his legs, they were moving so fast.

'You're the real champion dancer,' they cried. 'You're

number one!'

So they brought Dyaydyu over to make their plans.

'When we have our big dance tonight,' they said, 'you will lead the dancing. For tonight we'll put those two turtle sisters right down in front, because they have good voices to accompany the dance. You'll be dancing up and down, and when you come close to those two sisters, sitting down in the front row, you must kick them hard to make the water come.' That night was the biggest dance of all. Everyone came together, and the whole mob of them began to clap and shout and chant. 'Hmph, humph, humph, . . .!' They clapped and stamped on the ground. Emu, and Porcupine, and Goanna all led the dancing for a while. And those two Dugul sisters sat down in the very front row, singing.

Pretty soon Kangaroo Rat began to lead the dancing. He started dancing up and down, coming closer and going back again. All the others were singing out and clapping their hands.

Then Kangaroo Rat led a row of dancers right up close to where those two turtles were sitting. When he came very close he suddenly leapt out and kicked the Dugul sisters right in the loins, one after the other.

The water suddenly spouted up, out of their bodies, and it began to flow and flow in all directions. The water covered the ground. All the creatures clapped their hands, saying, 'At last! Here is our water!' They all sat down and began to drink. They drank and drank and drank. They drank until they were no longer thirsty.

Even today, at the place called Wuyii, there is a great swamp that never dries up. The water flowed out of that lagoon and created creeks and waterholes in every direction, which are still there.

Before all the creatures returned to their homes, the sea animals and the land animals exchanged clothing with one another.

Crocodile and Goanna traded skins. Crocodile wanted Goanna's tough hide because he lived in the water.

Sea Urchin traded his hard spikes with Porcupine, whose soft spikes were better suited to the sea.

Many snakes and fish traded with land animals, too. Even the big sea turtle, Ngawiya, traded shells with the land tortoise. He wanted to get rid of his big heavy shell, because he was going back to live in the sea. But Tortoise was in such a hurry when he got his new shell, that he put it on back to front. And even now that Tortoise has his shell on backwards, with the pointed end up at his head.

Afterwards all the creatures returned to their homes. The creatures of the land all went outside, back to their own camps. The sea creatures all swam down the great river that had been created when the swamp was formed. That's the very river that we still call Nguudhuurrbigu.

51

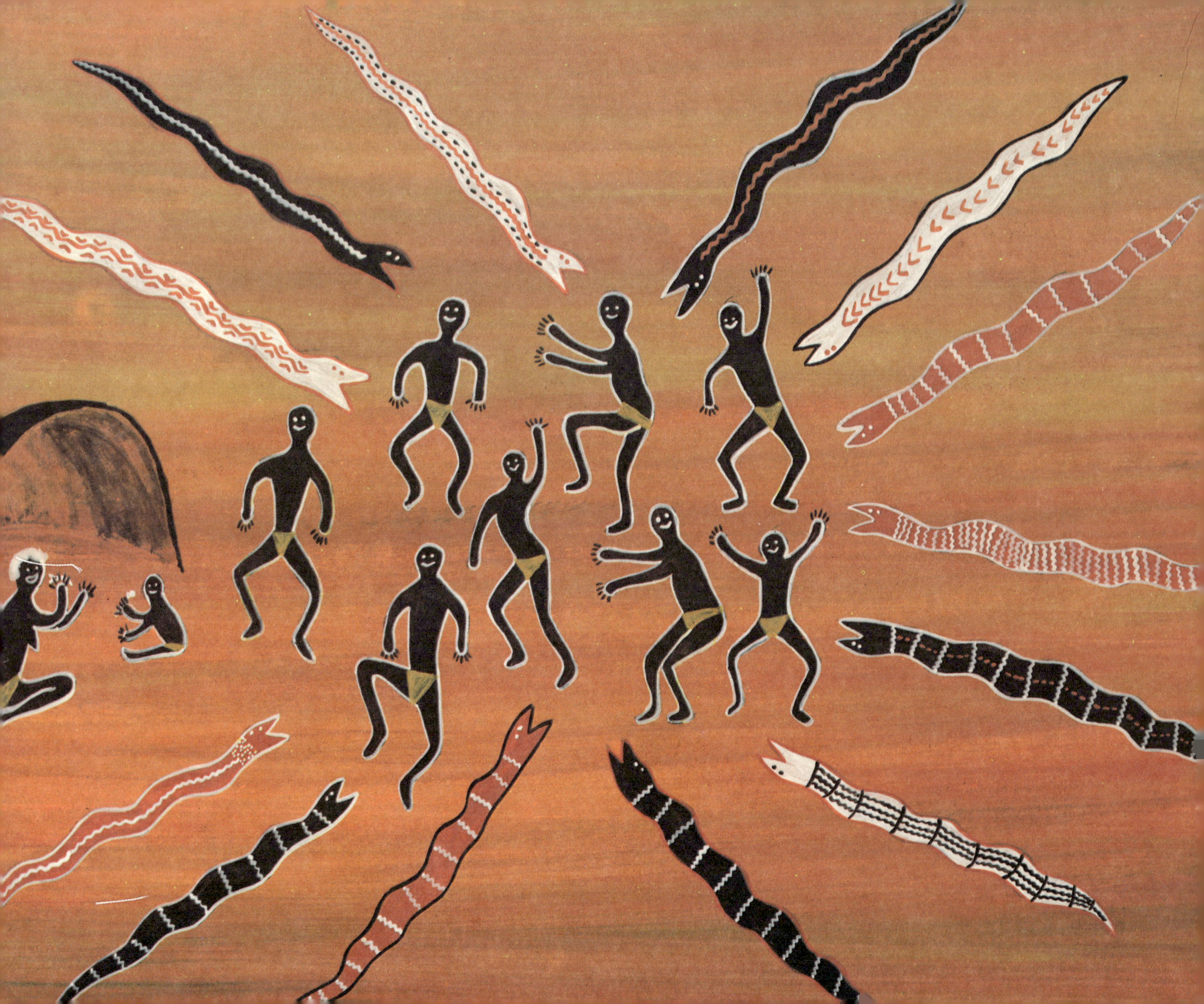

The big dance and the angry old woman

A long, long time ago, all the different Aboriginal tribes came together for a big corroboree. They came from the East, from the West, from the North and from the South. They gathered and sat down, and said to each other, 'Let's have a great dance.' And they agreed that the dancing would go on for many days and nights.

Of a daytime, all the dancers used to go out hunting. They would kill meat, and gather different kinds of yams – gaangga and wugay – and wild bush honey, called mula. In the evenings, when they came back to camp, they would cook the food they had gathered. And they would all sit down together and have a big feed. They would eat and eat and eat until their bellies were full. Then they would get up and start to dance. They would dance all night long. And this went on for many days.

In that same camp lived an old woman and her young grandson. They lived off to one side, by themselves. Every night, before they began the corroboree, and after they had eaten their fill, the dancers would take the bones and skin from the game they had killed, and bring it over to that old woman and her grandson to eat.

In time, that old woman got very cross with the dancers, because they gave her nothing but skin and bones.

One day when all the others had gone out hunting, that old woman took her pointed digging stick, and went with her grandson down to the river. It wasn't long before she killed a yidi, a spotted stingray.

The two of them went back to camp and cooked that yidi, in the ashes of the fire. When it was ready, they took it out, and sat down to eat all the meat. When they had finished all the flesh, they took the skin and bones that were left over. Then the old woman stood up, and began to throw pieces of skin and bones from that stingray all around. She threw some to the North, some to the South, some to the East and some to the West.

The two of them got up, and they ran off to the mountains. They went into a cave to hide.

After a while, the giant supernatural snakes – we call them yiirmbal – began to smell the skin and bones from the stingray that the old woman had thrown about. They all started to come out, heading for the place where all the dancers were. All the snakes from the land and the sea started to come out. Some travelled on the surface of the land; others travelled underground. Some came up the rivers. And they came from all directions, towards the big dancing ground.

The dancers saw all those giant snakes coming after them.

But where could they run to? With that big mob of snakes coming from all sides, there was no chance of escape. Some people got swallowed up where they stood. Others ran off towards the hills, where the snakes caught them.

Now old Frill Lizard didn't know what to do or where to hide. He saw those snakes coming after him, and he looked all around to find some way to escape. Suddenly it occurred to him to go right up in the sky and hide in the clouds.

Before he went up, though, he looked around and picked out a great heavy stone, just in case. He carried that stone with him when he climbed up to the clouds.

When he got up in the sky, Frill Lizard started looking down below to see what was happening. He saw a giant green snake travelling up the Endeavour River. So he leaned down and sang out: 'Watch out, watch out! I'm going to drop this great heavy stone!'

But that green snake didn't pay any attention.

So Frill Lizard let go of that big stone, and it dropped down, down, and crashed right on the back of the big green snake. Well, even today that big rock still sits in the middle of the Endeavour River, and people see strange looking animals on it.

All right, but what became of that old woman and her grandson?

Frill Lizard was still up in the clouds when old Dharrmali, the Storm, came up from the South. Storm came up to Frill Lizard and he asked, 'What's going on here? What are you doing up here in the clouds?'

Frill Lizard told him, 'I came up here because I was afraid of all those giant snakes.' And he told Storm the whole story, about the dancers, and the old woman who threw the pieces of stingray around to call the snakes out.

'Those two caused all the trouble,' he said, 'and everybody is getting swallowed up by the snakes. I only just managed to come up here to this cloud.'

'Hmmm,' said Storm, 'and where are those two trouble-makers now?'

'They ran away,' said Frill Lizard, 'and who knows where they went!'

Then old man Dharramali said, 'Just let me go have a look for them.'

He began to search around, here and there. He searched and he searched. Finally, he caught a glimpse of some fresh footprints leading into the cave on the mountain side. He picked up a few of his thunderbolts and watched the cave. After a bit, that old woman just poked her head out of the cave to see what was going on. Old Storm grabbed his thunderbolts and he struck that cave, again and again. Lightning flashed and thunder roared, and both the old woman and her grandson were killed.

Frill Lizard then went to find a long, long piece of lawyer-vine. He sent it down, down, into that cave, until it hooked that old woman and the child. Frill Lizard took the two bodies and threw them way out in the deep sea.

And that was the end of those two troublemakers.

Behind the Myths

Tulo Gordon is an Australian Aboriginal from the Hopevale Mission, near Cooktown on the Cape York Peninsula in northern Queensland. His people, speakers of the Guugu Yimidhirr language, once occupied a large area stretching from the Annan River northwards to the Starcke River, and inland for more than sixty miles. The stories translated in this book are Tulo's versions of traditional tales from his native territory. The stories mostly centre around the Endeavour River, whose mouth forms Cooktown harbour. These tales give accounts of the formation of prominent features of local geography, or the origins and habits of local species of plant and animal. On the other hand, the stories provide moral lessons about proper social order among Guugu Yimidhirr people in traditional times.

The people who produced these tales lived in a rich and complex environment, both natural and social. Their stories represent a striking intellectual and aesthetic effort to bring natural facts into harmony with a human order. More importantly, this collection of stories, told and illustrated by an individual like Tulo Gordon, represents another sort of an effort at reconciliation: Tulo Gordon has recalled tales from an era of Aboriginal life long-since vanished, and he has recast them in words and pictures that derive from a life still current. The stories survive, then, as a legacy from a Guugu Yimidhirr society obliterated by the European invasion of its territory, passed on to the Aboriginal descendants of that society, now living in a drastically altered world.

Like other Australian Aborigines the Guugu Yimidhirr people of the Endeavour River area lived by hunting and gathering. They were accomplished at spearing and trapping game, large and small, as well as fish. They used a variety of spears, each tailored to specific sorts of prey, with different wood or stems as shafts and a wide range of materials – bone, rock, quartz, stingaree barbs, and so on – as spearheads. They used a broad spear-thrower, called a *milbiir*, shaped something like a sword with a hook, to give added force and leverage to the throw. They had as well a detailed knowledge of edible plants, and of the seasonal rhythm that governed, among other things, the ripening of yams, the maturing of the edible water-lily root, the profusion of the wild plums, or the annual return of *dhuga*, the scrub hen, to her permanent nest to lay eggs.

The entire area inhabited by the Guugu Yimidhirr people could be thought of as divided into small territories, each with its own name, and containing distinctive named places. Each territory had, also, a principal family – a group of brothers, perhaps, with their wives and children, or an older man with a collection of offspring, both married and unmarried – who 'belonged to that place'. Such people had first claim to the native foods that grew in the territory, as well as proprietary rights to its sacred places. For example, Tulo Gordon's father – and hence Tulo himself, although he has in his lifetime never had the opportunity to exercise his rights – 'belonged' to an area called Nugal Dyin.gurr. Nugal is a mountain between the right and left branches of the Endeavour River known in English as Mt Harris; the word *dyin.gurr*, which means 'younger sister', distinguishes Tulo's country from Nugal Gaanhaal ('older sister'), which lies on the other side of the same mountain. Although his people did not cultivate 'bush tucker' so much as collect it, Tulo points out that they had both an intimate knowledge of what he calls 'nature' – the whereabouts of edible plants, their timetables, and so on – and also exclusive rights to enjoy its fruits. It is because of such exclusive rights that Fog grows angry at the theft of his yam by Thunder; he is enraged by his son-in-law's digging not of a yam that he has planted but of one that grows on his land.

There were also wider human or social needs that went beyond matters of food, and that transcended local territorial boundaries. Guugu Yimidhirr people from widely separated locales gathered together from time to time for ritual occasions. For example, large groups celebrated the transition of a group of youths into adulthood. Such initiation rituals were themselves connected with food: a time and place in which a certain yam was plentiful and mature was, for example, appropriate for the ritual which transformed boys into full men who were, in their new adulthood, for the first time permitted to eat that species of yam. When people gathered together for a large ceremony, which might last for weeks, it was no simple matter to feed the multitudes. Often the proceedings had to be suspended, as in the stories here about great dances, so that participants could take time to hunt and gather food.

According to Tulo Gordon, Aborigines in the early days were 'strictly law-abiding people' who 'had their own laws', particularly relating to marriage and proper demeanour. A man could be severely punished, even speared, not only for poaching on another's territory, but also for marrying 'crooked' – that is, marrying someone who was too closely related or who stood in the wrong sort of kinship relationship. In a kind of mock or symbolic battle, a man contracted to marry a woman, often when she was still a child, by subjecting himself to a lengthy beating by his prospective parents-in-law, receiving on the head several heavy blows with a spear-thrower which left blood streaming down his face. People were also constrained from disrespectful behaviour with their in-laws, their parents, and blood relatives of the opposite sex. In the most extreme case, a man was not supposed to speak at all when his wife's mother was in earshot; ordinarily he avoided her presence altogether. There were also special polite words, used in place of ordinary Guugu Yimidhirr words when speaking with people who required special respect (a man's father-in-law, for instance). Breaches of etiquette, a disrespectful word, or a misplaced joke might, in Tulo's words, cause someone 'to pick up a spear and kill you one time'. Tulo recalls that people who transgressed rules of proper conduct, especially in relation to sexual affairs, were often given animal nicknames like 'dingo' or 'porcupine' to underline the fact that they had disregarded the laws governing human conduct and hence were more like animals than people. (In the honey story, Frill Lizard suffers when he incautiously handles his sister's *yirrbi*, her skirt or loincloth, which subsequently becomes permanently stuck in his throat.) Serious transgressions – wife-stealing or murder, for example – might also result in a ritual spearing; the culprit, defended only by a champion wielding a shield or spear-thrower, was encircled by a group of men who tried to spear him in the thigh or buttocks, if not to kill him outright.

On the other hand, a man who proved himself to be *burrba* – brave, strong, and a good hunter – might often have more than one wife. Frequently the parents of the first bride would give such a successful provider a second or third daughter. (In the stories, too, co-wives are usually portrayed as sisters.) A good hunter was called *mala minha* (which means something like 'adept at getting meat'), and such a man was clearly an asset not only to his immediate family but also to all the members of the group with whom he lived. For, as Tulo puts it, Aborigines used to live 'the commonest way': they shared food within a given group, each individual being entitled to some specified part of another's kill. Shares were not necessarily equal, however, and although women accounted for a large part of a family's food with their gathering activities, a good deal of the larder found its way into senior male stomachs. (The old woman, given a supply of food and left behind to die, in the story, seems to represent an actual practice in traditional Guugu Yimidhirr society. However, as the old woman who summoned the supernatural snakes demonstrates, in another story, not all women and children given the leftovers and bones were satisfied with their treatment.)

Foods of different types were also subject to dietary laws, some species being reserved for certain classes of people (only initiated men, for example, could eat a particular type of white yam), or prohibited to certain classes (e.g., pregnant women). The way in which game was killed also affected its edibility. Tulo remembers, as a lad, watching an older brother surrender a giant barramundi because he had mistakenly speared it with his uncle's spear. As a result, according to Tulo's mother, none of them could eat it, and an elder man in the camp made a feast of it all by himself.

Not surprisingly, for a people who depended for their existence on a detailed knowledge of their surroundings, Guugu Yimidhirr people were (and still are) marvellously observant and well-informed about the physical environment, master bushmen who note subtle differences between species of plants and animals and who know how to take advantage of their particular properties or habits. They distinguish, for instance, hundreds of varieties of fish, stingrays, birds, marsupials, and lizards. Consider some of the reptiles that figure in the stories: for example, the *mungurru*, or bush python. Compared to the *gabul*, or carpet snake, *mungurru* is less brightly-coloured and 'less cheeky'; it won't bite! Both snakes are strong and determined hunters who will cause small birds to set up a commotion, to 'laugh' – a sure sign by which men know that the snake is near. Among the poisonous snakes, which abound in north Queensland, although none is as poisonous as the *biigaar*, the taipan, people reckon *walanggarr* the death adder to be the most deadly. Rather than taking flight when disturbed, this snake tends to hide itself in sand, waiting, almost invisibly, to bite an unwary foot. (Walanggarr thus is the appropriate choice, in the story, to watch from his hiding place when the two Dugul sisters sneak off to drink their water in secret.) Another talented reptilian spy is the ubiquitous Frill Lizard, a peculiar-looking animal (whose swollen neck, we recall, derives from his greedily swallowing his sister's loin-covering, dipped in honey). When you try to catch a glimpse of him on a tree, he always scurries to the opposite side, keeping his frills flattened and his legs down, so as to stay out of sight. Perhaps the most imposing reptile of all, around the Endeavour River, is the *ganhaarr*, the salt-water crocodile. Guugu Yimidhirr people considered him to be almost human, travelling great distances from one river mouth to another, fiendishly clever, strong and dangerous, preying, as in the story, particularly on women whom he desired as brides. In the early days there were crocodile-hunting specialists, who dared to dive into a known crocodile's haunt to wrestle with him and kill him. Even in recent times people have lost their lives to crocodiles, and Aborigines talk of the creatures with respect.

The Guugu Yimidhirr people exploited their environment with simple but often ingenious technology. The raw materials were all around. Different woods had individual virtues: some were especially hard, suitable for clubs and spear-throwers; some wood was strong and could be straightened in the fire to make a spear; the soft wood of the *bulal* tree was ideal for firesticks. *Midal*, the lawyer-cane, had useful (and often inescapable) barbs; the *yuulnga* nut contained a stringy fibre for twine; tea-tree bark made excellent tinder and versatile wrapping material; a pointed kangaroo bone was the perfect needle or spear-tip; a clump of *baaydyin*, a coarse grass, served as a sponge for sopping up soup or wild honey; and so on. Before Europeans invaded the territory, Guugu Yimidhirr people did not boil food, but used instead a variety of complex cooking techniques. Large game was often roasted in an earth oven, called a *gurrma*, which used hot stones and red-hot chunks of clay from ant-beds for heat. On to these was piled the meat, and the whole was covered with leaves and dirt. Smaller game, as well as cakes or pudding-like foods made from yams, nuts or grain, were cooked in the ashes of the fire. Preparing some foods, for example the *badhuurr* nut from the *zamia* palm, involved days of pounding and rinsing out toxic juices, before the pulp could be formed into a cake and roasted. (No wonder the spirit in the story was so jealous of his store of cakes, not wanting the water rat to steal them away after he had spent so long in their preparation.)

Taking advantage of the resources the land offered required extensive knowledge of terrain and territory. In the rainy season, one needed to locate shelter and fuel; in the dry, one had to know about permanent sources of fresh water. Significantly, many sites mentioned in these Guugu Yimidhirr stories are places where fresh water is to be found: swamps, springs, a waterfall, and main camping places along the rivers and creeks. Other places have remarkable features for which the stories give accounts: around the waterfall where the water rat lived are great stones, in the shape of cubes, which appear almost to have been cut by hand and stacked one on top of the other like so many gigantic cakes. Are these, perhaps, the remains of the wudhi's stockpile of zamia cakes? At Nobby Point, where in the story the bush python is petrified by the sun, the rock shows a curious scale-like formation, and walking along the point is, indeed, something like treading on the back of an enormous serpent.

These stories also deal with some of the less tangible entities in the Guugu Yimidhirr universe. Tulo remembers from his childhood hearing about many different kinds of ghost and spirit, some denizens of forest and scrub, others frequenting water. Spirits of dead people, called *wudhi*, were particularly dangerous, capable of possessing human beings and driving them into mad frenzies or fatal depressions. Another female ghost, called *dyiliburu*, travelled about with a basket, reaching out with her long rubbery arm to snatch unguarded infants from their mother's very laps. Forest spirits, like the *diimuur* with his ten beautiful daughters, could also trap unwary hunters, calling them from the treetops, and causing them to throw their spears wildly or injure living human beings. Other creatures, less man than beast, also populated the scrub. There were terrifying monsters like the *manu-galga-dhir* (the 'spear throat'), hapless humans transformed into great hulking globs of flesh, capable of emitting thunderous roars and thumping the earth so loudly that trees shook and the ground trembled. Supernatural forces appear and reappear in Tulo's tales. The curse has a peculiar power, and just as an old witch can, in the stories, blow on her victim's ear to produce a transformation, cave paintings in Tulo's home country depict men or women 'with a funny kind of a face, or a funny kind of a leg or foot'. Such a painting, Tulo remarks, was 'going to make that man sick'. Guugu Yimidhirr people do not now paint such figures, but many still express a healthy respect for the possible efficacy of a spoken curse or a verbal charm.

The supernatural creature that appears most often in these stories is called *yirmbal*. Tulo has explained to me that 'yirmbal could be anything': a giant snake or eel, a huge fish, an enormous shark, or perhaps something more nebulous, a shapeless creature that inhabits and protects a waterhole, a swamp, a mountain or an outcropping of rock. Sites known to be inhabited by yirmbal were dangerous, and in some sense sacred to the people who belonged to the territory involved. At Nobby Point, where the great python turned to rock, Aboriginal fishermen in the early days used to speak in a whisper, asking the yirmbal who inhabited that place to guide their turtle-hunting efforts. The creatures protected an area, but were liable as well to send punishment to human evildoers. A camp to the north of Cape Flattery, in the Guugu Yimidhirr area, was known by older men in Tulo's youth to have been obliterated, literally swallowed up by an angry yirmbal displeased by the inhabitants' faults and misdeeds.

Tulo Gordon's stories derive, then, from this universe, divided socially and geographically, peopled by human beings and other creatures. Most of the stories depict a time, long in the past, when, as Guugu Yimidhirr tradition has it, *all* living creatures were human, to be changed one at a time into animals, birds, spirits, or heavenly bodies, as a result of their deeds and propensities.

Some of the stories Tulo learned as a child from his mother or auntie, some from his older brother, the late Major Mango, who spent a long time as a boy in the company of 'free' Aborigines in the bush. Others he heard, as he grew up on the Lutheran Mission at Cape Bedford, from old men from different parts of the territory, men like old William, Darkan, Barney, or Charlie Burns, Charlie Maclean or old George Bowen.

In Guugu Yimidhirr these tales are called *milbi*, a word that signifies not only a traditional story or legend, but also a piece of news, a tidbit of gossip, or an account of recent or past events. And although Tulo heard many of these tales at his mother's knee, they are clearly something more than children's stories: they were meant to entertain and edify adults as well, to point to social morals, or to surround familiar places and things with an aura of significance and a depth of tradition. More than this, these stories *belong* to a place and a people in a way that goes far beyond our attachment to fairy tales. Not only do they spring from the Guugu Yimidhirr landscape, but they represent an era of the past of Tulo's people that no longer exists, and, indeed, that survives only as a childhood memory for the oldest people still alive today. For a people whose culture was dismantled, whose land was taken, and whose lives were, as we shall see, deformed and carefully controlled by a conquering, alien European population, these stories represent a link with an Aboriginal world now vanished. What is more, the stories make sense; they still work. Tulo, marvelling at the logic and clarity of the tales, often remarks on how clever the old people were to put such stories together. The stories 'go straight through' and 'they make you think'. The Aboriginal creation of a world in which animals talked, hunted, ate, and married like men is, Tulo says, something which he is sure Aborigines 'didn't pick up out of white man's ways'.

Still, it must be clear that the stories we have written down here, really come 'from the past'; in Tulo's words they are 'as told to me, not by book, but by spoken words'. These tales are not some mystical, sacred tribal property, nor are Tulo's versions the only full, true, or correct ones. They represent one man's collection, learned from many people, often in only fragmentary or half-remembered form, then embellished or regularised in Tulo Gordon's head. Many tales from the Endeavour River have counterparts elsewhere in Australia. Tulo knows, for example, that stories about the origin of water (here hidden by two turtle sisters) or a ferocious giant dingo dog (in the Guugu Yimidhirr version owned by an ill-tempered python) are 'spread right over' northern Australia. One danger in writing the stories down here is that they will be taken as more than they are meant to be: just one selection of good stories that belong to Guugu Yimidhirr *bama*. We have left out many other good stories, that tell how Moon murdered his own son, or how the grasshopper, the grass, and the water became friends, or how the *balin.ga* (porcupine) got his quills: spears thrown by his irate kinsmen after he made improper advances towards his own sister.

Although in the English versions we have tried to keep both elements of Guugu Yimidhirr storytelling style and the special flavour of both Guugu Yimidhirr and Hopevale English phrases, there is a fundamental difference between a story, written, punctuated, and spaced on a printed page, and a tale enacted by a gifted storyteller (like Tulo Gordon), complete with dialogue, drama, and sound-effects. These stories are meant to be heard, and Guugu Yimidhirr people deserve to have them recorded and published in their own language. Needless to say, the translations draw as heavily upon Tulo Gordon's English as on his Guugu Yimidhirr.

This book, however, represents something more than a collection of stories from a group of Australian Aborigines. For, whatever the original contexts in which these stories were told, and whatever the interdependencies between these tales and traditional Guugu Yimidhirr society and environment, the present collection represents a rather different expression of Aboriginal life, in a modern context. It is in fact miraculous that the stories (and the storyteller) have survived at all, let alone the community of Guugu Yimidhirr people to which they belong. The fragmentary nature of the collection, the hybrid language in which the stories are retold, and the salvaged remnants of tradition and lore around which they revolve all give forlorn testimony to the fate of the original inhabitants of the Endeavour River. Tulo Gordon's own life can stand as a kind of miniature history of the restructuring of Aboriginal life in the Guugu Yimidhirr area.

Tulo Gordon was born about 1922 in a camp on the Endeavour, up river from Cooktown. His father, Charlie, was the last of several brothers and sisters from Nugal Dyin.gurr to survive the invasion of his territory by gold miners, sugar planters, settlers, bêche-de-mer fishermen, and policemen, and to remain in his homeland. Tulo's mother Minnie came from an area called *Dyuubi* (known in English as Boiling Springs). She was known by the name of her long-time employer, a settler named Gordon. She worked for years, before and after Tulo was born, sweeping house, washing clothes, and doing other domestic chores for white people around Cooktown. Old Charlie had been a handyman, a stockman, a goatherd, a police tracker, a labourer in the cane fields, and, as Tulo says, was 'well-known to white people'. But Tulo's family was not tied, as were many local Aborigines, to a particular property or station; they still moved from place to place, camping for some months with other Guugu Yimidhirr people at 'Two-Mile' on the Cooktown-Laura railway line, moving up the river to Stonewall and other camps, or across the wide mouth of the Endeavour River to the North Shore Reserve, where Aborigines who laboured during the day in Cooktown were sent to camp at night after the curfew banned them from town. Cooktown was by this time only a skeleton of the goldrush boom town of the 1880s that grew up to serve miners bound for the Palmer River goldfields.

When Tulo was born, his father, though still given on occasion to going 'on the walkabout', had begun to work regularly for the Lutheran Mission at Cape Bedford, some fifteen miles up the coast from Cooktown. The Mission had begun a cattle operation at an outstation called Spring Hill. Tulo's family lived in a bark shelter, while his father and the white stockman rode the fences, and rescued stock from bogs, swamps, and cattle-duffing neighbours. Tulo's older brother Major and two sisters were already living permanently at the Mission, called Hope Valley, boarding at the school. Tulo's playmates were children from other nearby camps. Sometimes a boy from Bridge Creek, another camp on the mission reserve where non-Lutheran Aborigines were allowed to take refuge from the outside world, would spend time with Tulo's family. At the North Shore camp Tulo swam and played, and occasionally saw traditional dances, in the company of police trackers' children. People in the camps went hunting and fishing and gathered seasonal foods in the bush. But Tulo remembers most fondly the bread and rough cane syrup that he could wheedle at North Shore from people who earned money in Cooktown.

Life was uncertain for Aborigines around Cooktown at that time. Adults were free to roam about the land in search of game and food only so long as their movements did not annoy the settlers and their stock. Fishing boats landed randomly up and down the coast recruiting and abducting boys and women from Aboriginal camps. Aborigines were tolerated around settlements, or mining camps, and indeed were encouraged to work by white people, but only so long as they were tractable. Offenders were ushered from the area by police, deported to penal settlements in the south, where they would no longer be subject to the bad influences of their 'habitual haunts'. Thus did it come about that Tulo's uncles and aunts one by one disappeared from his world, as did the parents of his young mates. Those adults who remained increasingly sought refuge on the reserve controlled by the Lutherans, where the supply of flour, tea, sugar and tobacco was less reliable than on the outside, but where Aborigines could live with some small measure of autonomy.

Aboriginal children had fewer options. By the late 1920s, Tulo remembers, policemen used to go out to the camps and stations to find Aboriginal children of school age. Policemen 'used to muster 'em round and send 'em in the Mission'. The missionary at Cape Bedford accepted young children from the entire Cooktown area (and, indeed, from distant parts of Queensland as well), fed and clothed them, educated them, and brought them up as hardworking and serious Christians. Tulo and some of his age mates from Bridge Creek and North Shore were rounded up and deposited at the mission in the late 1920s. Throughout this period, police brought in children from the mining camps and sparse settlements further afield: from Laura and Coen to the West, from Port Stewart, Barrow Point, and Princess Charlotte Bay to the North. These children said good-bye forever to camp existence as they had known it, beginning instead a carefully regimented life of study, work, and worship.

The Lutheran mission at Hope Valley had been founded in 1886 by German missionaries, delayed on their way to New Guinea. After forty years of hard and determined efforts, the missionaries had created an enclave of Lutheran discipline, isolated in every way possible from outside society, both white and black. Many of the inmates, some part-European, were orphans or children forcibly separated from their parents before being sent to the mission. Others, like Tulo, only saw their parents on occasions when the dwindling numbers of camp people visited Cape Bedford for rations or work. The remaining children were mission-born, living at school while their parents worked at outstations. In any case, Tulo joined a society strictly divided into age groups, and carefully structured along Lutheran principles. The oldest Aboriginal people lived off the mission entirely or in small camps on mission territory but carefully segregated from the small Hope Valley congregation. Older Lutheran Aborigines, pupils from the early days of the mission, who had married other converts, worked the farm and fishing enterprises at mission outstations. The children formed groups according to their level in school: the oldest children who had finished their studies formed different work gangs. Other classes in school were hierarchically organised, older students supervising younger ones, and all under the strict and watchful eyes of the missionary and his family.

Tulo Gordon remained in school until 1938. He learned all the ordinary subjects taught in a rural Queensland school of that era: reading, arithmetic, poetry, spelling, composition. (Aboriginal children off the mission were lucky to receive any schooling at all.) He and his fellow pupils were diligent students of the Bible, accomplished at singing hymns in Guugu Yimidhirr. Tulo also learned about hard work, in the mission gardens and coconut plantations, and later on the mission boat, diving for trochus shell and bêche-de-mer. And it was at school, first following his brother Major's lead, and later encouraged by the schoolteacher, that Tulo began to paint. He drew animals and boats with charcoal on bark or driftwood. Later he used tins of paint, washed up on the beach, with homemade brushes. Encouraged in his early efforts, Tulo occasionally gave his sketches to other people at the mission who used them, along with Lutheran Bible pictures, to decorate their walls.

In 1942, the superintendent of the mission, a man in his seventies who had been at Cape Bedford continuously since he arrived from Germany in 1887, was arrested by the army and interned in a camp for German aliens. The inmates of the mission, seemingly contaminated by their contact with German missionaries, were summarily packed onto boat and train and evacuated en masse, and without warning, to Woorabinda, a settlement near Rockhampton. There they had, for the first time, unmediated exposure to Aboriginal life in a white man's world. Tulo went out to work on wartime manpower gangs, picking peanuts, harvesting arrowroot, cutting cane. The Cooktown people also fell victim to the diseases of colder climates. Tulo himself lay near death for several weeks in a Cherbourg hospital. Many of his countrymen succumbed; Tulo's brother Major had three children die of fever in the space of two days, in early 1943. Nearly a quarter of the Cape Bedford people died, and the nature of the community, always heavily dependent on kinship and family relations, was drastically altered as entire families were snuffed out.

At Woorabinda Tulo Gordon tried his hand at a variety of new things. He tried the guitar; he played football; and he continued to paint. When a new mission was opened at Hopevale, near Cooktown, the Cape Bedford people who had survived went north again. Tulo devoted himself to a new life in his own country, a life with changed rules. He built a house with his own hands (a house he still rents from the Queensland government), planted fruit trees and gardens (on land the mission apportioned), married a woman from Palm Island (where he and some other single men were dispatched by the authorities to find wives), and raised a family. (Tulo and his wife Gertie have had eight children, of whom seven are alive.)

But life at Hopevale is often onerous for Tulo and his countrymen. His brother Major Mango (who died shortly after the manuscript for this book was completed) was always restless at the mission, trying repeatedly to gain exemption from Queensland's repressive Aboriginal legislation. Tulo found the possibilities for employment at the mission restrictive and unrewarding. He again put his talents to work, producing carved wooden curios for sale at the mission shop. He tried bark paintings (which he does with his left hand) and landscapes (which he does with his right). With these bark paintings, not native to the Guugu Yimidhirr area at all, Tulo developed the style illustrated in this book. He began to reach into the stock of traditional tales that he and others at Hopevale remembered, depicting the old stories on bark, often writing summaries of them on pieces of paper and pasting them to the backs of the paintings.

This book is thus a natural outgrowth of Tulo's own effort to recapture and represent his people's stories in a modern context, rather far removed from his own life of fifty years ago, to say nothing of Guugu Yimidhirr society as it was before white men destroyed it. Just as the Guugu Yimidhirr storyteller used these tales to connect the natural and social world as he experienced it to a past moral order as he conceived of it, Tulo Gordon here presents bits of his own people's traditions to connect modern Hopevale with a distinctly Aboriginal past, a past cleansed of imposed European ways. But this book is clearly a product of the present. Hopevale Mission exists. What becomes of the Guugu Yimidhirr people, and of Aborigines in Queensland and throughout Australia, is a story that people like Tulo Gordon must have the right to compose and tell for themselves.